D0934688

The Little Saint

A Helen and Kurt Wolff Book | Harcourt, Brace & World, Inc., New York

Georges Simenon

The Little Saint

Translated from the French by Bernard Frechtman

Copyright © 1965 by Georges Simenon
Translation copyright © 1965 by Georges Simenon
All rights reserved. No part of this book may be reproduced
in any form or by any mechanical means, including duplicating machine
and tape recorder, without permission in writing from the publisher.
First edition
Library of Congress Catalog Card Number: 65–21035
Printed in the United States of America

This is a translation of *Le Petit Saint,*
first published in France in 1965.

Part One

The Little Boy
of Rue Mouffetard

I

HE WAS BETWEEN four and five when the world came to life around him, when he grew aware of a real scene involving human beings and was able to distinguish them from each other, to locate them in space, in a particular setting. Later on, he could not tell whether it had been in summer or winter, though he already had a sense of the seasons. Probably in autumn, for the curtainless window was dimmed by a slight blur, and the yellowish gaslight that came from the lamppost outside, which was the only light in the room, seemed humid.

Had he been sleeping? His body was warm beneath the blanket. He had not been abruptly awakened by any particular sound, he had merely heard behind the curtain, which was only an old bedsheet that hung from a rod, a familiar panting broken by moans, and from time to time the creaking of the bedspring. It was his mother who slept in that bed, almost always with someone. On his side of the hanging sheet were Vladimir, then Alice, then the twins, then he himself, each on his straw mattress, and, against the wall, the baby on her iron folding-cot.

Vladimir was a big boy, at least eleven and a half, if not more. Alice must have been nine, and the red-haired twins, who had freckles under their eyes, about seven.

The mattresses lay side by side on the floor and smelled of mildewed hay. The room was filled with other odors which were those of their home, of their universe, and there were also the odors of the whole house and, when the window was open, those from outside.

He had opened his eyes, not out of curiosity, but because he was awake. He had recognized the gleam of the gaslight on the ceiling and through the cloth partition. He had listened vaguely to the panting, then had gradually made out the figure of Vladimir, in a shirt, kneeling on his mattress and peeping through a hole in the bedsheet.

Louis was neither surprised nor curious. It was all familiar to him, as if he had often been through the scene without realizing it. But it was the first time that the images and sounds had ever merged into a meaningful whole.

"Alice!" whispered Vladimir, turning to his sister.

"What?"

"Are you asleep?"

"Almost."

"Look . . ."

She too was in a shirt. None of them wore night clothes, and they slept in shirts.

"What?"

Vladimir motioned to her to come to his mattress, and she in turn got on her knees and looked.

The twins were breathing evenly and did not stir. Emilie, the six-month-old baby on the cot that had been used by all of them, each in turn, did not yet matter.

Again he heard the muted though distinct voice of Vladimir, who ordered:

"Do it to me."

4

"Will you do it to me afterwards?"

Vladimir had lain down with his shirt pulled up above his belly.

"Be careful with your teeth."

Louis was so unmoved, so uninterested, that he dozed off. When he opened his eyes again, Vladimir and Alice seemed to be sleeping. The twins were still breathing evenly, but the kerosene lamp was lit in the kitchen, the door of which was open. A smell of coffee, spiked with brandy, floated in. Two persons were talking in the kitchen in low voices.

Wasn't it like that in every home, in every house, in every family?

His grandmother had once remarked:

"Louis hardly ever talks. He must be a little backward."

He did not remember who had answered:

"All the same, maybe he thinks about things. It's children like that who are often the most observant."

He had paid no attention because he did not know what it meant, but for some reason or other the words had stuck in his mind. There were others too, and particularly images, for even if he really was dull-witted he had not lived till the age of four without seeing what was around him.

But it was somewhat as if he had wanted to limit the world to as narrow a space as possible.

"If he were allowed to do as he liked, that child would never go out of the house."

Had he actually heard that comment or had it been repeated to him later? It's not easy to distinguish between what really happened at a particular time and what you were told later on.

He was sure that the hole in the hanging bedsheet and the business of Vladimir and his sister were a part of real life, despite the vague glimmer from outside. He had seen his brother and sister do the same thing at a later time, in broad daylight, without bothering about him.

5

There had been a father in the home, a man named Heurteau, Lambert Heurteau, whom he had never known, except from the lone photograph tacked on the wall of the room. He was oddly dressed and was standing next to the children's mother, who was wearing a white dress and a veil.

Lambert Heurteau was not the father of all of them. How old was Louis when he discovered that in most families the children all had the same father? Not in theirs. And not in others on Rue Mouffetard, where they lived.

His mother's name was Gabrielle Heurteau. Her maiden name was Cuchas. As for the eldest, his real name was Joseph Heurteau, but Louis did not realize until much later, when he went to school, why he was called Vladimir.

Alice's name was also Heurteau.

"It's hard to know who she resembles. In any case, all you have to do is look at her eyes and that sharp nose of hers to tell that she'll go far."

"Unless she runs a pushcart in the street like her mother and grandmother."

The twins were Heurteau's too.

"They're the only ones he couldn't disown!"

Why hadn't Louis known the man in the photo and why was he himself called Cuchas? No one seemed to wonder about it, and for years he didn't either. Later, when he knew, he felt completely indifferent.

What mattered most, at first, was the two rooms in which they lived, more exactly the bedroom and the kitchen. During the day, the bedsheet which hung from copper curtain-rings was pulled back, revealing, on the left side of the window, a very high walnut bed, its two mattresses, its coverlet, and the huge quilt.

The image was vague, but Louis would have sworn that he had seen his mother in that bed surrounded by other women, that she had screamed a lot while they kept him in the kitchen

6

and that later they showed him an ugly baby and informed him that he had a new little sister.

His grandmother was present too. He saw her as a very fat old woman whom everyone called Ernestine.

Had he too been born in the walnut bed, and had he sucked his mother's breasts as he had seen Emilie do? Nobody called her Emilie. It was a long time before he knew her name. They simply said "the little one," the way they said "the twins."

"You twins, let the little one alone! Go out and play."

Much later, and only when he had become an adult, was Louis to remember other images that had not registered consciously and which, perhaps because they had to do with his daily life, had not struck him at the time.

The walls of the room had formerly been papered, but all that remained was patches on which there were still pictures of persons dressed as in the time of the kings. On one of the patches, near the door, was a young woman with very wide skirts who was on a swing. The rest of the wall was dirty, yellowish plaster on which were initials that had been carved with a knife and pictures representing genital organs which someone had tried to rub out. Who had drawn them? Who had tried to efface them?

Not his mother, in all likelihood. When the weather was warm, it didn't bother her in the least to walk around naked in the room and even in the kitchen. When she had not yet put up her big red bun, her hair hung down to her waist, and the bush at the bottom of her slightly plump belly was very fine and fluffy, of the same light shade as Alice's hair.

She was cheerful and often sang while doing the housework, when she had time to do it.

The straw mattresses were covered with a thick, rough brown cloth, except Vladimir's, which was bluish. The only sheets were on the wooden bed and the enameled cot.

"Alice! Go warm your sister's bottle."

"Why is it always me?"

Who had given *him* the bottle?

The twins were only three years older than he, and he was four and a half years younger than Alice. Was Vladimir eight when Louis was born?

These questions did not yet occur to him, except a few, the simplest ones, which did not disturb him, because everything seemed natural. Later, much later, he was to wonder how such and such a thing had happened when he was a child on Rue Mouffetard, but it was out of idle curiosity, a kind of amusement.

It was in 1897 or 1898 that he had observed what his sister was doing so docilely to Vladimir, though it did not interest him enough to prevent him from going back to sleep. It did not surprise him that his mother wore a high corset which left marks on her fine, soft skin, or to see some men wearing caps in the street, others bowlers, and others silk top hats. He had heard it said that the family was poor, but wasn't everyone in the building poor and almost everyone on the street, except the storekeepers, such as his Uncle Hector who ran a butcher shop at the corner of Rue du Pot-de-Fer?

"If he hadn't been a fast talker and a good-looking boy, he wouldn't have got around the Lenain girl. Besides, the family let him have her only because she limped. All the Lenains have something wrong with them. The grandfather ended up in an asylum, and as for Azaïs's brother, God knows what he died of. It wouldn't surprise me to learn that Hector, even though he is my brother, had a hand in it . . ."

She laughed. His mother laughed as often as she sang. When she was in bed with a man she began by sighing and moaning, but it always ended with a burst of laughter.

She got up very early in the morning, at times, in summer, at three o'clock. She would wash her face in the kitchen, where there was a copper faucet. In winter, she lit the fire before

8

leaving. Louis would sometimes hear her. At other times, when he woke up he would see that she was no longer there.

He knew that she went to Les Halles, the central market, with her pushcart, which she had rented from a certain Mathias who had a yard full of them on Rue Censier, to stock up on fruit and vegetables. At six o'clock she was at the curb, facing the shoe store, while his grandmother installed herself about a hundred yards lower down the street, near Saint Médard's Church.

At the age of four or five, he was unaware of all that, or rather it was part of a world which was not his, which was only remotely connected with his daily reality.

For example, the stove was, for a long time, more important than his mother and was the focal point of his existence. He did not yet know how it was lighted, or by whom. All he remembered was that his mother, who would be out of breath from climbing the stairs, would cross the room with a bucket of coal whose weight tilted her to the right.

There was no door between the kitchen and the corridor. You had to go through the room. Louis did not mind the fact that their home had only one exit. It was reassuring, because he felt safely shut in, just as he was safe in the blanket at night when he wrapped it around his body.

The stove, which was next to the sink, filled a good part of the kitchen.

"We're lucky to have water on our landing. There aren't many people on the street, even those who are lots richer than us, who have water in their apartment. If only we had gas too . . ."

He knew what gas was, for in the evening he saw its pale illumination in the stores across the street and in certain apartments. It was even installed in the yard of the building, or rather in the carpenter's shop.

From his mattress Louis could hear sulphur matches being struck. He liked the smell of them. Then, almost always, his mother would sigh and mutter words that he could not make out, and the smell of sulphur would be followed by that of kerosene, which drowned it, and the new smell in turn was drowned by that of kindling wood and coal. He could have got up to take a look. He did later, around the age of six or seven. Until then, he preferred the mystery of the fire as it appeared to him from his bed, and since it was celebrated very early in the morning, almost always when it was still dark, he would fall asleep again before the end, before the jet of steam spurted from the kettle and the drops that fell one by one into the coffeepot changed the smell of the apartment once again.

He was told later when they had tried to put him into a nursery school when he was two years old, that he had not cried but had struggled, and that when his mother had left he had escaped by the window. As he still did not know his house from the outside, he had wandered about among the pushcarts and a policeman had finally gone up to him.

"What are you looking for, little boy?"

"I'm looking for Mama."

"Where is your mama?"

"I don't know."

"Have you lost her?"

"Yes."

"What's your name?"

"I don't know."

"You don't know your name? Don't you know where you live?"

"No."

He was wearing a little smock, the kind worn at the time by boys his age, and his hair came down almost to his shoulders.

"You're not a girl by any chance, are you?"

"No. That's my sister."

He had only one, for Emilie had not been born yet.

"What does your father do?"

"I don't have one. I want to go home."

The policeman, it seems, had taken him from store to store.

"Do you know this kid?"

The storekeepers examined him more or less closely and shook their heads.

"Do you live in the neighborhood at least?"

"I don't know."

Finally, he had caught sight of his mother behind the pile of vegetables in her pushcart. Or rather, as the story was told to him, his mother had caught sight of him walking hand in hand with the policeman.

"What are you doing here, Louis?"

"I don't know."

"How'd you manage to get out of school?"

"I don't want to go to school any more."

"Germaine, would you mind my cart for a moment?"

She had taken him back to the house where the twins were sitting on the kitchen floor playing with blocks. These were not memories of his own. He was unable to remember so far back.

"Even when you were six, they had a devil of a time keeping you in school. You refused to learn . . ."

Perhaps it was not so much that he refused to learn as that he refused to be taken away from the universe which he considered his own and in which he felt safe.

He liked the room that was divided in half by the bedsheet which hung from a rod, he liked the smell of the mattresses lined up side by side, the portrait of his mother in a white veil and of a man with a blond mustache, the patches of wallpaper, particularly the one with the girl on a swing. He liked, above all, the warmth that the stove gave off in waves, in blasts, the way it roared at times, the glowing ashes that suddenly collapsed into the drawer at the bottom.

"Your son doesn't talk much!"

What would he have said?

. . .

He must often have tried later, at different ages, to recon-
stitute the successive stages of that birth of the world around
him. Not because he attached any importance to the matter. It
was only a game, though a secret, voluptuous game.

He never quite managed to link them up. Images were missing, particularly pictures of himself, for the only photograph he
knew was the wedding photo of his mother and Lambert Heurteau that was on the wall. The latter had one hand on his wife's
shoulder, and the other, which was gloved and holding the other
glove, rested on a pedestal table that fascinated Louis for a
long time, until the day he ventured beyond the neighborhood
and discovered an identical table in the shop of a secondhand
dealer.

Why did it seem to him, when he contemplated the ill-lit
face and pale blond, drooping mustache of that man he had
never seen, that he was dead?

"But he's not, idiot. If he were, Mama would be a widow
and we'd be orphans."

"Me too?"

"Not you, since he's not your father."

"Why?"

"Because he went away long before you were born."

"Why?"

Perhaps because he had been fed up. Or because their
mother had been.

That conversation took place several years later, when he
was about eight or nine and dared ask Vladimir questions.
Vladimir continued to despise him, but now took the trouble
to answer him condescendingly.

"Did they fight?"

"When he drank, or when Mama drank. Haven't you ever
heard Mama fight with the others?"

"Did he beat her?"

12

"Sometimes. Mama was stronger than he and he always ended by getting the worst of it."

"How do you know?"

"Because I used to look through the hole, and I listened when they drank in the kitchen."

Vladimir had adopted a defiant attitude. He outstared everybody and never gave in. He was the only dark-haired member of the family and was taller and more nervous than the others. His long eyelashes fluttered about his dark pupils.

"I don't give a damn . . . He's not my father. Mama was pregnant before she knew him. My real father was a Russian and I heard someone say he was an anarchist."

"What did he do?"

"He prepared bombs and set them off."

Before that, Louis must have discovered one of the two monuments of their apartment, the sink and faucet, which were almost as important as the stove. On Sunday mornings their mother, who did not work that day, put up water to heat in a huge laundry tub.

She had to ask M. Kob, their neighbor, to help her set the tub of almost boiling water on the reddish tiles in the kitchen. M. Kob did not have to be asked twice, for Gabrielle had nothing on under her dressing gown and generously displayed her breasts when she bent.

At that hour, on Sundays, he smelled of cosmetics and wore a gauze appliance to set his black mustache.

Alice, because she was a girl and was less dirty, got into the tub first. She was soaped from head to foot, with her hair hanging in wet locks on her cheeks and hunched shoulders.

Then it was Vladimir's turn. He insisted on washing himself without anyone's help.

"Don't forget to wash your ears."

"I'll wash whatever I like."

Then came the twins. At times it was one and at times the

other who was first. In the street and at school they were called the redheads, and other children were afraid of them because they were always looking for a fight. At home, on the other hand, they acted indifferent, as if they did not feel they were members of the family. They had violet-blue eyes and very pale skin, and almost every winter they came down with the grippe together.

"Your turn, Louis."

The water was already blue and slimy with soap. It did not disgust Louis to be fifth. He was never disgusted. Not by the smells either. Was anyone in the house or even in the street disgusted by smells?

There were no toilets on the landing. And neither the arch nor the yard nor the stairway was lit up, so that the most important object in the room was a heavy white crockery chamber pot. Everyone used it, the mother first, and also the men who came to see her, who sometimes lived with them for a month, sometimes for a few days, sometimes only for a night.

"Hell! The damned chamber pot is full again!"

This one was a coachman who brought back two bottles of red wine in the pockets of his box-coat every evening. Gabrielle and he did not go to bed immediately. They would sit in the kitchen, which was lit by the kerosene lamp, and, with their elbows on the table, would talk in low voices as they drank their wine. When the mother started laughing, it meant that before long they would be going to bed.

She would lower the wick, which went out a minute or two later, and the room would be lit only by the street lamp opposite the window. Since they lived on the first floor and Rue Mouffetard was not a wide street, it was rather light in the room. The man, in his shirttails and long underwear, would lift up the pot that the children had filled.

"Hell! This God-damned chamber pot . . ."

He would open the window and empty it on the sidewalk

while Gabrielle howled with laughter. She herself poured it into the kitchen sink and then let the water run. The coachman had been with them for almost a month. One Sunday he piled them into his hack and took them to the Bois de Boulogne. Emilie, who must have been a year old, sat on her mother's knee. Vladimir was perched on the high seat and before long was using the whip.

For years, it was their longest trip. Actually, they never took another one together.

Of course, Gabrielle left for Les Halles very early with her mother and other peddlers, each pushing her cart. But when the local market began, at the curb, she spent the rest of the day about a hundred yards from the house.

When Emilie was very little, Alice looked after her, and it was also she who filled the stove and stirred the fire. From time to time, their mother would ask a neighbor to mind her pushcart for a few minutes.

"Here! Put up this meat to cook with onions and a dash of vinegar."

The meat did not come from the shop of her brother, "Hector the millionaire," as she called him.

"Ever since that lousy pimp married his cripple and became a boss, he's forgotten that his family ever existed."

At heart, she did not hold it against him. She was rather proud of him. Isn't that the way things always happen in families, and wouldn't she have done the same in his place?

She had another brother, Jean, who was a bit feeble-minded, a lamplighter who went by in the evening with a long pole at the end of which shone a small flame for lighting the gas lamps and who went by again early in the morning to put them out.

"A loafer's job. And yet he was the only one of us who went to school till he was fifteen."

All of this had registered in bits and pieces. Louis never seemed to be listening. What he heard was always mingled with the hubbub of the street, especially in summer when the two windows were open, the one in the kitchen and the one in the room.

"That one's not interested in anything."

Perhaps it was true. Nevertheless, certain phrases, certain intonations were filed away in his memory without his bothering to put them in order, to link them up, to try to understand.

"And yet he looks intelligent . . ."

Because of his smile, most probably. A gentle smile, without irony, without meanness, without aggressiveness, a smile that someone once compared to that of Saint Médard, whose church stood at the bottom of the street.

He was happy, he watched, he went from one discovery to another, but, unlike Vladimir, he made no effort to understand. He was content with contemplating a fly on the plaster wall or drops of water rolling down the windowpane.

Certain drops, for example, which were bigger and muddier, caught up with the others by taking a short cut instead of zigzagging. At times, this went on for hours, against the background of the huge red boot with a gilt tuft that was the signboard of the shoe store on the other side of the street.

The storekeeper was M. Stieb, and his name, which Louis was unable to read until much later, was elegantly written out in cursive style on the two windows that framed the narrow door. Louis could see people enter, especially women with one or more children, and it was fascinating to watch them gesticulate without hearing their words. M. Stieb had a square beard and wore a detachable wing collar, a purple four-in-hand, and a frock coat.

He invited the mothers and children to be seated, got down on his knees to remove the youngsters' shoes, and then began to play a game with boxes, which he went to take from the shelves and from which, with the gestures of a conjurer, he removed shoes of all shapes.

The mother, who held a shopping basket on her lap, would shake her head: no.

"Wait! Wait! I've got just the thing. How do you like these?"

"No . . . No . . ."

No patent leather. No kidskin. Good solid thick-soled shoes, preferably with hobnails!

At the left, in the semidarkness, thin, severe-looking Mme. Stieb would look on with an air of indifference. She was homely. The redheads called her a sick hag.

She was buried a year or two later. Everyone on Rue Mouffetard, including the peddlers, went to the funeral. The shutters remained drawn for three days. When M. Stieb reopened them, there was a saleswoman in the store.

The shutters were fascinating too. Those of the shoe store were lowered with a crank that fitted into a small hole in the shop front, and in summer another crank lowered a red-and-yellow-striped awning, the edge of which stopped just above the heads of the passers-by, so that the tall ones or those who wore a top hat had to stoop. Another awning, a solid gray one, obliged them to do the same in front of the tripe shop.

The storekeepers did not all shut up shop at the same time, and the grocer, who had only one show window, but whose store stretched depthwise, was the last to put up two wooden panels which he wedged with an iron bar and then locked before doing the same with the door, so that he had to leave by way of the blind alley.

Louis spent hours at the window, as he did in the yard watching the carpenter in his glass-fronted workshop. M. Floquet was a tall thin man who stopped sawing or planing from time to time to roll a cigarette.

He probably was not rich enough to hire an apprentice, and when he needed someone to lend a hand in order to hold two pieces of wood together, he would call his neat and tidy wife, who emerged from the kitchen in a starched apron.

When, in spring or summer, part of the glass front was open, a good smell of glue and fresh wood emanated from the shop, though the odor was spoiled a little by that of the building's only toilet, whose door, on which someone had sawed out a heart, was ajar day and night, revealing on the ground a dirty crockery slab with two places for the feet and a hole in the middle.

Beyond the yard opened still another world, for the building was very large. Though all the tenants were more or less poor, those whose windows overlooked the street were the privileged ones. Among them were even people like M. Kob, who, when he went out, always wore a bowler, sometimes a top hat, and almost always a frock coat. People said he was a laboratory assistant at the medical school and that it was he who cut up the corpses which were not claimed by relatives.

Nevertheless, even in that part of the house there were more old people than young, widows and widowers, especially widows. Some of them received a little help from their children, some had savings, others were on the rolls of Public Assistance, and at least three of the tenants on the upper floors were no longer able to go down the stairs.

A kind of tunnel led to the second yard, where the garbage cans were lined up. At night, cats and, so it was said, rats too would knock down the not properly placed covers. A stairway, whose bottom steps were of stone, though the rest were wooden, led out to the right. The iron banister was supported by bars that were too far apart, and several children had been hurt. One of them had fallen down two or three flights and had died.

Not everyone spoke French. There were a little girl and her brother who had almond eyes. A tall, thick-lipped Negro lived with a tiny little woman whose skin was as pale as that of the twins. Louis would sit on a step and watch. He rarely asked questions. When his mother came home alone for a meal, she was too busy with the others, and almost every evening there was a man in the room, sometimes a stranger, most often someone who stayed rather long and did not mind playing with the children, as the coachman had done.

Vladimir was the only one who could have cleared up certain points, but he looked at his brother so haughtily and with such contempt that Louis preferred not to ask him anything.

Yet Louis could have denounced him. Vladimir had got into the habit of bringing home in the evening things that did not belong to him, candy and chocolate which he munched in bed before going to sleep, coins that he hid in his mattress, a penknife that shone as if it were made of silver, and even a lady's watch that he would sometimes put to his ear before going to sleep.

One day Alice discovered the watch, and when Vladimir got home she dangled it in front of his nose at the end of its chain.

"Where'd you get this, Vladimir?"

"Let me have it."

"Only if you get another one for me."

"I'm ordering you to let me have it."

"And I'm warning you that if you don't give it to me, I'll tell Mama. And I'll also tell her that you look through the hole and make me do what she does."

"She doesn't care. Let me have the watch."

"I won't."

"I promise you I'll give you another one."

"When you do, I'll give this one back to you. Is it gold?"

"It's plated."

"Is it fake?"

"It's not fake, it's plated. It's almost as good as gold. Listen, Alice . . ."

"I won't."

Vladimir then turned his rage on Louis.

"What are you doing here?"

"Nothing."

"Were you listening?"

"I heard."

Vladimir went to get the penknife, which he opened with a meaningful gesture.

"If ever you make the mistake of talking about it to Mama or anyone else, I'll puncture you. You know what that means?"

"I do."

"Come here."

"No."

"You'd better."

Vladimir stepped forward, grabbed Louis's wrist, pulled up his sleeve, and, with a quick stab, dug the point of the blade into his skin.

"Does it hurt?"

"It does."

"Well, if I really stab you, it'll hurt even more, and they may have to take you to the hospital. Do you remember the man they found on the sidewalk last month with a knife in his belly?"

The people who got up early had seen him from their windows, for he had lain in the street more than an hour without help.

"All right! So keep your mouth shut. Get it?"

"I get it."

And Louis walked away from his brother with a smile.

II

WAS HIS MEMORY playing tricks, was it an optical illusion? He had the impression, later, that his childhood had been a succession of periods of discovery, of intense activity, and of periods of somnolence of which he had no recollection, except of a kind of general tonality, sometimes a grayness, sometimes a sort of luminous fog.

The same went for his contacts with people. Some of them seemed, for a time, to have disappeared from his life, though he had continued to see them every day, whereas others, for no apparent reason, entered the foreground, and in such minute detail that they seemed ridiculous.

Such was the case of M. Stieb, whose gestures and facial expressions were so deeply engraved in his mind that he remembered when the shoe-seller had clipped his beard and when he had changed the style of his detachable collars.

Thus, from his first-floor window he followed, without trying to understand, goings-on which for him had no importance but which must have had an enormous amount for M. Stieb. The new saleswoman was dark-haired, full-breasted, and broad-hipped, and she had a well-rounded behind. She dressed strictly in black, as if she too were in mourning. Was she a widow, or a member of the family, Mme. Stieb's younger sister?

In the beginning, she served the customers and knelt in front of their stockinged feet, juggled cardboard boxes, climbed up the ladder that slid along the shelves.

Formerly, when there was no one to wait on, M. Stieb would stand at the door of the shop and make pleasant remarks to the women who stopped in front of the show windows.

But now, as soon as he had a free moment, he would disappear with his saleswoman into the back of the shop until, a few weeks later, he started waiting on the customers as he had done before, while the buxom young woman sat in front of the cash register.

Louis did not remember the marriage, which must have taken place during one of his periods of apathy. Nor did he ever know whether Vladimir stole another watch for his sister. At the age of about five, there was a void of several months of which almost nothing remained, except an impression of sun and heat, of the smell of fish and other food that rose up from the street.

Vladimir, who was thirteen, would return from school with a school bag that he tossed into a corner, near Emilie's cot, but Louis never saw him open a textbook or notebook, nor heard him talk about his class or teacher or schoolmates, whereas the twins sometimes sat face to face at the kitchen table doing their homework and learning their lessons.

They were all different. Except for the fact that they lived under the same roof, usually ate together, slept on mattresses that lay side by side, and washed in the same water on Sunday, there were few contacts among them.

Vladimir had black hair, which was thick but fine, with a lock that fell over one eye.

The twins, who were more square-faced and bonier, had their red hair cropped close.

Alice was blonde and fragile-looking, and her chest was beginning to swell a little around the nipples.

Louis could not see himself. The only mirror hung too high on the wall for him and was used only by their mother when she put up her bun.

Louis was short, he knew it, shorter than the other boys his age, and his hair was even finer than his sister's.

As for Emilie, she was beginning to walk in a kind of pen that was set up for her during the day with the mattresses.

Why was Vladimir more present to his eyes than the twins, of whose doings over a long period he had no recollection at a later time?

That summer his mother cut his hair, and he was surprised to see her wrap one of the curly locks in a piece of tissue paper. But though he remembered the lock and the tissue paper, he had no memory of the operation itself and could not tell on what chair or where in the apartment he had sat.

He was discovering Rue Mouffetard, where he was beginning to walk around by himself, with his hands in his pockets. As he saw it, the street was divided into two distinct parts.

To the right of his house, on the way to Place de la Contrescarpe, stores were not so closely huddled together. There were fewer dark alleys between the houses and few pushcarts along the curb. It was a foreign world.

In the other direction, toward Saint Médard's Church, the street became denser, more swarming with people, full of noises and smells, of the cries of peddlers, of piles of food, and of refuse in the gutter.

He often went to see his mother, whose green pushcart he recognized from a distance. On sunny days, it was covered with a piece of canvas that was held up by two sticks and bits of cord.

"Take a look at my lovely peaches, Madame . . . Don't be afraid . . . There's none like them in the whole market . . ."

The stock changed every day: peaches, plums, lettuce, string beans.

"Monsieur, try my Williams pears . . . Come! Don't be shy . . . Your wife won't scold you . . ."

A slate was stuck at the top of the pyramid, and between the shafts of the cart was a small board that supported the scales and the metal container.

His mother hardly had time to talk to him. The members of the family never talked much.

"Is Alice with your little sister?"

He wondered whether Alice had ever been to school. His mother would give him a piece of fruit, in other seasons a stalk of tart rhubarb, a few thick-shelled, fuzzy beans, and sometimes a sou. He would walk down the street, jostled by the crowd, stopping at the fish market to look at the heaps of mussels and shrimps and green-eyed fish.

At times he would have to step over a man, unshaven and in rags, who lay sleeping across the sidewalk beside a pool of vomit.

He never went beyond the church, which was his frontier, and he took no interest in the carriages and omnibuses that rolled by with a clopping of horses' hoofs.

His only expedition beyond the neighborhood, when the family had piled into the coachman's hack, already seemed unreal to him. He had seen the Seine flowing, churches, huge buildings, wide streets with silent houses where there were no pedestrians, avenues, and carriages drawn by two and even four horses in which young women, dressed in white, toyed with their parasols. He had caught sight of horsemen in shiny boots, officers with gold epaulettes.

No doubt it was all very beautiful. His mother went into raptures.

"Her whole dress is real lace and she's wearing enough jewels to buy half of Rue Mouffetard . . ."

He was unimpressed. For him, it was outside of reality, and he had finally dozed off.

The Dorés, opposite the window, were more real and for a time played an important role in his life. They lived on the first floor, above M. Stieb's store, but their apartment was not like his. It contained at least four rooms, maybe five or six, for Louis could only catch a glimpse when the door happened to be open.

The floors were so brightly waxed that the sun played on them as on a pane of glass, and in certain places they were covered with multicolored rugs in which dark red predominated.

Mme. Doré and her husband were old. They were at least fifty. In summer, their three windows stayed open all day, and a young housemaid in a white apron and white cap would beat the rugs and carpets over the sidewalk.

Did other residents of the street have a maid? Mme. Doré wore a corset which was so stiff that it made her look like a statue. Her tight bun, which was still black, had streaks of gray. She was never seen in house clothes. Her dresses, with wide leg-of-mutton sleeves, were of colors hard to describe, violet, for example, with mauve glints, or oak-leaf brown or even lavender-blue.

The two front rooms were the dining room and living room, and when Mme. Doré sat down to breakfast she was already fully rigged up, without a hair sticking out, wearing a white or black tucker that made her keep her head straight and hold up her chin.

Lots of little dishes and utensils with which Louis was unfamiliar lay on the white tablecloth, and almost every day Mme. Doré shook a little bell to call in the maid and tell her to put such and such an object in its right place.

M. Doré was fat, had broad side whiskers, and wore, at home, a snuff-colored jacket with frogs and braiding.

They almost never seemed to talk. He would read his newspaper in a velvet armchair. His complexion was florid, and after every meal his wife would take a decanter from the sideboard and serve him a little glass from which he drank while smoking a cigar.

They were the landlords of Louis's house and also of the house in which they themselves lived, to say nothing, so people said, of four or five other buildings on the street. In summer, when M. Doré left the house he wore a pearl-gray frock coat and was very careful not to soil his patent-leather shoes by walking in the rubbish. He invariably carried an ivory-headed cane, and his eyes were always sad.

It was the Dorés who, in the past, had run the hardware store a little farther down the street which had been established by Grandfather Doré, who had started as a blacksmith.

For Louis, the Dorés were linked up with his sickness and that of his brothers and sisters. By cross-checking, he later established the fact that he was about five and a half at the time. It was after a hot summer, most of which he spent in the street.

After that, there had been a series of storms, one of which was more violent than the others and had transformed the sloping street into a torrent, and as the sewers had overflowed, the street had reeked with a foul stench for several days. Workmen and firemen had even come to dig a trench in order to repair the damage.

When the storms were over, the rain had persisted and got colder every day. He did not know whether it had been in October or November. In any case, they had started lighting the fire in the kitchen stove and the windowpanes were covered with steam. He had made drawings on them with his fingers.

One night, Louis had a stomach ache and went to the chamber pot twice. In the morning, he felt very warm and his eyes itched.

He had not spoken of it to anyone, because it was not unpleasant. He had even gone out for a moment in the morning and had seen M. Doré, who was wearing an overcoat and carrying a rolled umbrella instead of his cane.

"Aren't you eating?"

"I'm not hungry."

"Have you been on the pot yet this morning?"

"Once."

"Was it liquid?"

"I don't know. No. Not too liquid . . ."

"If it continues I'll ask the druggist for a remedy."

No doctor, as far as he knew, had ever set foot in their apartment. He knew the one who treated almost the whole neighborhood, for he had often seen him go by with his medical bag. The doctor was a round-shouldered man with a white goatee who was always dressed in black and dragged along as if he were dropping with fatigue.

The mother went, instead, to the druggist, who would ask her a few questions and sell her a syrup or a powder to be diluted in water or whitish pills that melted on the tongue when you couldn't swallow them and which then left a bitter taste.

"Louis, are you sick?"

Alice was minding the little girl. She never complained about all the things she was asked to do. Nor did she ever play. She wasn't sad, but the expression on her face wasn't the same as that of other little girls.

"No. I only had a bellyache."

"You're all red."

He could feel that his skin was getting hotter and hotter, and he went to the window to cool his forehead against the pane. He felt hot and cold. It was both pleasant and unpleasant. He would have liked to lie down, but he didn't dare to, for if he were really sick he would be taken to the hospital. Though no one in the family had ever yet been there, he did occasionally hear it mentioned:

"Say! The fishwoman's little boy is in the hospital."

"What's the matter with him?"

"They don't know. It seems to be something in the head."

From time to time, an ambulance would stop at the curb. Men in white would enter a house carrying a stretcher and come out with someone on it, usually an old man or old woman. He had once seen a woman struggling to free herself and screaming:

"I don't want to go there . . . I won't . . . Help! . . . Don't let them take me . . . Maria! . . . Hortense! . . . Help! . . . If I go, I'll never get out and I'd rather die at home . . ."

Louis had witnessed the scene without turning a hair. The only person who had commented on the incident was a little old woman.

"I understand her, poor thing. No doubt they take better care of you there, but I feel the same, I'd rather die in my own bed too . . ."

Louis did not want to go die in the hospital and he said nothing that evening, though he had the impression a number of times that the walls were spinning around him. He had nightmares. He felt that he was huge, that he was getting huger and huger, as if he were being blown up, until he filled the room, and he floated.

He did not know how he had floated, but he had lost contact with the floor and was begging them to hold on to him, to help him get down.

When he woke up, his blanket was damp. He felt drained. His mother had left for the market long before. It was broad daylight and no doubt she was already at her place beside the curb with her pushcart. Alice, who was sitting on the mattress of one of the redheads with her chin in her hand, was looking at him in a way she had never done before.

"Am I red?" he asked anxiously.

"No. On the contrary. You're all white."

She seemed sunk in thought and kept staring at him.

"Are you hungry?"

"No."

"Would you like a bowl of coffee and milk?"

He didn't know. He didn't feel like having or doing anything. Or rather he would have liked to go back to sleep, for his eyelids were heavy and swollen, and he felt bone-weary.

"Do you want it or not?"

He nodded. He heard her moving about in the kitchen, while Emilie crawled on the floor, pushing a tin can. Alice came back with the bowl, helped him sit up, and, when he protested, said to him gravely:

"You've got to do as I say. I'm your nurse. If you don't obey me, you'll die."

His throat was tight. He tried to drink, but before he had drunk half the bowl he squirted the liquid.

"You can see that you're very sick. If they took you to the hospital, they'd probably open your belly, the way they did to a little girl I know. They took out a lot of pus and then they sewed her up again. She showed me the scar. It's as long as that. It seems they've got a room there full of coffins for those who die . . ."

She suddenly seemed much older than he, and he did not doubt the truthfulness of what she was saying. She spoke with the detachment of someone who knows but can't do anything about it.

"I'm not sick."

"You are! You're very sick."

"It's not true."

"It is. I'll take care of you."

"What are you going to do to me?"

He already saw her opening his belly with a kitchen knife or a pair of scissors.

"I'll ask the druggist for a medicine."

"You won't say anything to Mama?"

29

"Where'll I get the money?"

"There's probably some in Vladimir's mattress."

"Do you like Vladimir?"

"I do."

He liked everyone, even the twins, who never paid any attention to him except to make fun of him. They claimed he was too short, that he wouldn't grow up, that when he was old he'd be a tiny little man, maybe a dwarf, like those who lived on Rue du Pot-de-Fer.

"I don't like him."

She added, while removing, without surprise, coins and unexpected objects from her brother's mattress:

"He's cruel. Sometimes, instead of sucking me, he bites my pisser . . ."

He did not see her leave, did not remember what happened afterwards. When he opened his eyes again, his mother was in the kitchen. There was no man with her. The kerosene lamp was lit.

He felt he had a damp, warm dressing around his chest and stomach, and he had difficulty breathing, probably because the dressing was too tight. In spite of himself, he started groaning, and his mother knelt beside him while the others continued to sleep.

"Does it hurt?"

"No."

He tried to push aside the dressing.

"I'm choking."

"Don't touch it. It's good for you."

She had put her cool hand on his forehead.

"You're already less warm. You're going to drink a little broth I've prepared for you."

He wasn't hungry, only thirsty, thirsty for very cold water, but he was forced to drink the broth with a spoon. He was so tired that all he could think of was going back to sleep, but he had strength enough to ask:

"Why is everything wet?"

"Because you did it twice in your sheets and I had to wash your mattress."

It lasted two days. He learned this only afterwards. His grandmother spent one of them in the house, and she too made him drink broth with a spoon. As soon as he opened his eyes, he made sure that he was in their room, still fearing they might have sent him to the hospital. He also made sure that the old doctor wasn't there. Once, he caught sight of Vladimir looking at him, somewhat the way Alice had done, as if he were expecting to see him die and were curious to know what would happen.

"Does it hurt?"

"No."

"Are you cold?"

"I'm hot."

"But yesterday you were shivering and your teeth were chattering."

"Did the doctor come?"

"What for? Would you like a chocolate?"

"No."

He added:

"Thanks."

For it was the first time that Vladimir had ever offered him one of the candies that he swiped from stands and of which he always kept a supply. He was filled with tenderness for Vladimir, for Alice, for the twins, for little Emilie whom he neither saw nor heard, as her cot had been transferred to the kitchen.

The others, the big ones, were strong enough to defend themselves against contagion. At one age or another they had all had the same thing, fever, stomach ache, diarrhea.

"Thanks," he repeated more gravely.

He would have liked his mother to be there too, and his grandmother, he would have liked them all to be around him, for it seemed to him that they formed a unit, that they were different from other people, that they alone, all together, had the power of defending one of their members.

He felt very small. The redheads were right. If he lived, if they helped him live, he would remain the smallest in the family.

He was only a child and he was almost frightened at the thought of being a grownup someday. His mother would be old, as old as his grandmother. Perhaps she would even be dead.

As soon as Vladimir grew up, he would go away and they would never see him again. Then the twins would go away. Why did he think they would marry the same woman?

He himself could marry Alice, so that she would always stay with him. He was afraid of being left alone. If they left him alone, he would die.

People were talking in the kitchen as if he couldn't hear. There were the voices of his mother and of a neighbor, an old woman who lived in the next house. She was a cleaning woman and smelled bad.

"All that's necessary is to moisten his dressing, as warm as possible, every two hours, by diluting a soupspoon of dry mustard and a handful of bran in a little water."

Then his mother spoke:

"I've got to go back to work. What with the rain, I've hardly made anything all week. If something happens, Mme. Gibelin, let me know right away."

"You can rely on me, Mme. Heurteau. Work is work, and I can understand you, I who've worked every day of my life."

. . . If something happens . . . If something happens . . . If something happens . . .

Maybe he was dying, since he no longer felt anything.

He never knew how long his sickness had lasted, nor exactly what it had been, for it merged, not only in his own memory, but in that of his brother and sister, with the sickness of the others. One day, Olivier, one of the twins, returned from school in the afternoon and complained of a headache. A little later he began vomiting. Gabrielle came home. She made him drink a cup of herb tea, which he threw up, and despite his pleading she wound a damp dressing around his torso.

It was midwinter, since, the next morning—Louis was sure of it—he was kneeling on a chair watching the snow fall, and on the other side of the street Mme. Doré, whom he saw indistinctly in the light and shade, was pensively contemplating the same spectacle.

It was an extraordinary period, for while Louis was getting better and regaining his strength, Vladimir announced, with an evil look at his brother:

"That does it, you've passed it on to me too . . ."

Because the children were sick, Gabrielle overheated the apartment, and the chamber pot was emptied into the toilet in the yard ten times a day. Gabrielle was obliged to work, for, as she said, only rich people can buy bread on credit.

Mme. Gibelin came for only two or three hours a day and spent most of her time looking after Emilie. Guy, the second redhead, joined his brother on the row of mattresses.

Louis could remember his mother leaving her pushcart for a moment, rushing up the stairs, feeling the children's foreheads, preparing a compress or distributing spoonfuls of a sticky syrup, and then going out again with her knitted woolen shawl tightly drawn over her chest.

"Louis, come and get me if anyone needs me."

For he was now the healthiest of the lot. His hair, which was finer than ever, was more curly. He spent most of his time looking out of the window or watching the gleaming ashes drop into the drawer of the stove.

Alice was less sick than the others. She too shivered with fever, and at night she uttered moans, at times actual cries, and seemed to be trying to push someone away.

Little Emilie crawled about on all fours from one room to the other, playing with anything, sucking whatever she could lay her hands on. No one realized that she had fallen sick too. She did not look ill and did not complain. She was put to bed, as every evening, in her cot, and as she did not wake up in the morning, Gabrielle leaned over her and then realized she was dead.

Mme. Gibelin, who arrived a little later, went to buy a bottle of cognac in the grocery store three houses away to buck their mother up, and she herself drank quite a glassful.

"You have to notify the district office. They'll send the doctor."

Louis did not cry and was not really sad. His main feeling was one of surprise.

It was he who had started the series, and it was the youngest of the children who died of the sickness.

The comings and goings that followed disturbed his tranquillity, and he was annoyed with the people who came in, looked at the little girl's white face, uttered laments, gave advice, related personal memories, and asked whether there would be a funeral service in the church.

The old doctor came too, for the first time, with his medical bag. What struck him most was the hanging sheet that isolated the wooden bed.

He sounded the chests of Alice and the twins, without knowing that Vladimir was hidden in the kitchen closet. He asked questions with an air of resignation, like a man who had seen and heard everything. How had it begun? . . . With Louis? . . . "Is that Louis? . . . Stick out your tongue, my boy . . . Don't be afraid . . . So you were the one who was sick . . . Did you have a stomach ache? . . . Did you have to move your bowels often? . . . What did you give him, Madame? . . . Did you put damp compresses on his chest? . . . Good . . . Didn't he have headaches? . . . Did he recognize you? . . . Who had it next? . . . Your tongue . . . Can you swallow easily? . . . Did you have a stomach ache too? . . . And then your brother? . . . Obviously . . . Obviously . . . These children ought to have been isolated the very first day . . . I'm not blaming you . . . In any case, there's no room in the hospital and they wouldn't have been able to admit them . . . And you, little girl, do you feel better? . . . I bet you began by taking care of your brothers . . ."

He looked about for a table, something on which to write, and it was in the kitchen that he wrote out the death certificate and then, as a measure of precaution, a prescription.

"Isn't it you who sell vegetables on a pushcart a little way down the street? I've seen you before. You work in the neighborhood, don't you? I think my wife often buys from you . . ."

When the body was put into the coffin, the children, whether sick or not, were locked up in the kitchen. Louis expected that there would be hammer strokes and was disappointed at hearing only the conversation between the carpenter and his assistant. It wasn't the carpenter downstairs, but another one, a more important one, who made coffins only.

Had Emilie spent that night with them? He did not remember, just as he had no recollection of other things that were more important than those that had stuck in his memory. In any case, the funeral took place on a windy, freezing morning. The neighbors, who were waiting in the street, held their hats in their hands, and the women's skirts stuck to their legs on one side and waved like flags on the other.

Vladimir was well enough to go out, for he disappeared a little later and did not come back until it was dark. Gabrielle returned home slightly drunk, accompanied by her mother, who tried to force her to go to bed with a hot-water bottle.

"I'm so afraid you may have caught cold at the cemetery . . ."

"No, Mama, it's not on a day like today that I'm going to coddle myself."

Mme. Gibelin had prepared a stew, and everyone ate heartily, even the twins, who were still running a temperature.

"The thing that consoles me is that she didn't suffer, and maybe it's better for her that she was spared this bitch of a life."

"Gabrielle!"

The grandmother was reprimanding her daughter, who, in order to pull herself together, was helping herself liberally to red wine.

"You're right, Mama. Why worry? Such is life, eh?"

It was not until much later that Louis learned these details, at second hand, from Vladimir, and perhaps Alice had not been wrong in claiming that Vladimir was cruel. One day, she too was to confide in Louis.

"You can't imagine what he forced me to do."

"I saw it."

"You mean when he looked through the hole and made me imitate Mama?"

"That's right," he admitted, blushing.

"That's not all. It made him sore not to be able to do it like the men, you understand? So he hid a big carrot under his mattress and stuck it into me. I couldn't even scream because of Mama and the fellow who was with her. I don't know how many times I bled and I had a burning pain for several days."

It would have been necessary to collate all the testimony. That was done, more or less, over the years, in bits and pieces, but Louis would merely listen halfheartedly, as if the truth about the others did not interest him.

He had not taken sides at that age either, when he was about six. His mother, who had once arrived unexpectedly during a fight between Vladimir and the redheads, had asked him:

"Louis, who started it?"

And he had answered quietly:

"I don't know, Mama. I wasn't looking."

He looked at lots of people and things, but not those in which he was expected to be interested. That same winter, he entered elementary school, after the term had begun.

His first day in the classroom, which was a turning point in his life, ought to have left an impression. He had not the slightest memory of it, though he very clearly recalled trying on blue-checked pinafores at Lenain's, the clothing store near which his mother set up her pushcart.

He remembered particularly the smell of the materials, the stiffness of the starched pinafore, and, a quarter of an hour later, the sight of M. Stieb, at close range, trying to fit him with high laced shoes.

"They wear them out so fast, M. Stieb! You'd swear they do it on purpose."

At that moment, he himself had wondered:

"Are M. Stieb and the lady smiling behind the cash register going to get married?"

They did get married, in the spring, discreetly, without a white gown and veil, and the shutters remained closed for the three days of their honeymoon.

On the long gray wall was printed: POST NO BILLS. Then there was a building of the same gray, two floors of classrooms, a short flight of worn steps in front of the building, a green door. The pupils did not enter by that door but by a small one in the wall of the yard. In the middle, the ground had been hardened by trampling. A band of paving stones two or three yards wide ran around the yard, and on one side was a covered playground for rainy days.

His classroom was on the ground floor. From his seat in the first row he could see the dark trunks of four chestnut trees. He had been placed in front because he was the smallest in the class.

"Are you sure you're six years old?"

"Yes, sir."

That wasn't the first day, but the second or third. On the first day he must have taken a seat anywhere, on an available bench. On the walls were a number of maps, though he did not know of what countries, for he had not yet learned to read, but he could contemplate the patches of different colors which were separated by sinuous lines, light blue, yellow, green, and particularly the purplish pink of the biggest patch.

There was a jumble of exciting lines on his desk too, the veins of the wood which stood out in spite of the black paint, and, in addition, the mysterious patterns that pupils had carved with penknives over the years.

"What are you looking at, Cuchas?"

"Nothing, sir."

Whenever the teacher called him by name, some pupil would burst out laughing, as if it were extraordinary or comical.

"What was I saying?"

"I don't know, sir."

For he had been taught to say "sir" whenever the teacher addressed him. That was not hard for him, since he was naturally polite and deferential.

"Weren't you listening?"

"No, sir."

"Why are you in school?"

"In order to learn."

"What have I put on the blackboard?"

"Strokes, sir."

"I want you to make the same strokes on your slate. Be sure that they're the same distance from each other."

He got down to work. He did not rebel, like Vladimir, and did not, like the twins, loathe school, where they were unable to break loose except during recess. The girls were on the other side of the buildings and had a smaller yard, without trees, for their recreation periods.

The big boys came running out at about ten o'clock, and before seeing them he heard the clatter of their hobnailed shoes on the stairs. The twins had already thrown a red rubber ball which the others tried to get from them, and they defended themselves energetically, throwing it back and forth over the others' heads and elbowing and sometimes kicking those who were about to get hold of it.

Vladimir was one of the biggest and walked around the yard with a friend whom Louis knew by sight because he was the son of storekeepers on the street.

He did not know their name. People said "at the Spaniards'." They had no show window. Their store was a kind of broad corridor, both sides of which were filled with displays of food, some of which Louis would often go to contemplate with even more admiration than envy.

For example, rough, hairy coconuts with a reddish tuft in the form of a goatee. Pomegranates, one of which was cut in two so that the customers could admire the color of the delicate flesh surrounding the pits.

He had never eaten coconuts or pomegranates or those tangerines which were preciously wrapped in silver paper.

The oranges were enveloped in crinkled tissue paper, and exotic-looking salamis, flat hams, and dates with plaited stems hung from the ceiling.

It all must have been good, tasty, different from what he ate at home, those little fish that were soaking in a tart sauce, those shrimp salads, those anchovies laid out in such neat circles in casks, the different kinds of nuts, the bottles surrounded with straw, the tin cans of all colors . . .

He was amazed to discover that his Vladimir was a friend of the Spaniards' son, of a boy who lived in the midst of so many good things and who no doubt ate them.

He too was dark-haired and had heavy eyebrows, and his lips were as red as those of a woman with make-up. The two boys kept apart from the turmoil of the others and seemed to be exchanging secrets. Louis could tell from the Spaniard's attitude that he admired and respected Vladimir.

"What are you thinking about, Cuchas?"

"I was looking at my brother, sir."

"At home you'll have all the leisure you need to look at him. Here you're supposed to work."

The young boys had recess after the older ones. When he in turn was in the yard, he had no desire to play with his classmates or make their acquaintance. The boy who shared his desk, who was also short, barely taller than he, and had a big red pimple on his forehead, went up to him.

"Why do they call you Cuchas?"

"Because it's my name."

"A name from what country?"

"I don't know."

"Don't you know what country your father's from?"

"I don't have one."

"You don't have a father?"

"No."

"Is he dead?"

"I don't know."

"Doesn't your mother know either?"

The question seemed to him so foolish that he shrugged. He had promised himself to go and look at the dark trunk of one of the trees which had a bump, like a big wart, and to run his hand over it. There were complicated patterns on the bark, like maps, but they were deeply carved and one could stick one's finger into them.

"Where do you live?"

"Rue Mouffetard."

"What does your mother do?"

"She sells vegetables."

"Does she have a store?"

"No. From a pushcart."

"Is your family poor?"

"I don't know."

It was true. He had never wondered whether they were poor. Actually, everyone in the building was poor. Even M. Kob, who dissected corpses and wore celluloid collars.

"Those people have to spend their money on clothes," their mother would say, "and I'm sure they don't eat as well as we do. Some of them try to act like ladies and gentlemen and then, after bargaining for a quarter of an hour, ask me if I don't have any leftovers."

"My father works in a bank."

This did not impress Louis, who did not know what a bank was.

"My mother doesn't work and we have a cleaning woman every Saturday. My two sisters go to a parochial school. Are you so short because you don't eat enough?"

"I've always been the shortest."

"Why?"

"I don't know."

He never asked himself the question.

After all, if he was always so calm and had a serene smile, perhaps it was because he did not ask himself questions.

"Too bad, because if a big fellow hit you, you wouldn't be able to defend yourself."

It was already time for the pupils to line up in front of the classroom, take their seats, and make pothooks.

III

THE TEACHER WAS a rather heavy-set, flabby, shapeless, color-less man named M. Charles. That was his family name. He was twenty-eight years old and unmarried. For reasons of economy he boarded with a widow on Rue Lhomond who mended his shirts and other clothes, which were never new. He had a child's mouth and almost no nose, and one could feel that he suffered from not being good-looking or able to aspire to a mini-mum of elegance.

From the very beginning, mysterious relations were estab-lished between him and Louis, as invisible, on the surface, as an electric current. It was a matter of neither sympathy nor antipa-thy. Perhaps, on the part of the teacher, whose only vanity, a rather naïve one, was to wear fancy vests under his ill-fitting, threadbare black jacket, it was mainly a matter of curiosity.

He taught two classes in the same room, the walls of which were pale green, and while the little ones were still making pot-hooks on their slates, the second group studied the multiplica-tion table and the history of the Gauls.

Louis applied himself, but without eagerness or enthusiasm. He did correctly what he was told to do and when his neighbor, the son of the bank clerk, left in the middle of the term to enter a private school, the teacher said to him:

"Cuchas, from now on I'd like you to attend to the stove."

The pupils all burst out laughing. Had the teacher done it on purpose? The stove, a big black cylinder six feet high, the pipe of which went through the ceiling, looked even more monumental when little Louis went to open its firebox and refill it.

Yet those were the best moments of the day. The school was not sparing of coal, as they were at home. Nor did it use little balls of grayish charcoal, but good shiny anthracite that burned with a clear bright flame. It was so beautiful, so fascinating, that Louis hesitated each time to close the cast-iron door.

In the yard, he did not play. He didn't feel like it. He stayed in a corner, watching, or digging up pebbles encrusted in the hard ground. The others would jostle him on purpose as they ran by. He sometimes fell his full length, and he would pick himself up without protesting, with neither ill-humor nor rancor, but with a vague smile on his lips, a kind of inner light in his blue eyes.

The two years in M. Charles's class went by so quickly that he was unable to tell later when he had begun to read and write.

For him, it was the trees and the yard that marked the flow of time. The trunks became less black, seemed less rough; then tight buds appeared at the ends of the branches. The sparrows chirped more often, and soon other unfamiliar birds appeared.

"What are you doing, Cuchas?"

The children had got into the habit of pronouncing his name with a stress that made it comical.

"I'm looking."

"May I ask what you're looking at with such attention?"

"The cloud."

A light pink and white cloud that remained suspended in the pale blue sky, right above one of the chestnut trees.

"I suppose it's interesting."

"It is, sir."

The pupils burst out laughing. It had become a game in which M. Charles participated by his unexpected questions, which he asked in a deliberately gentle, insidious voice.

"What is your slate used for?"

"For writing, sir."

The incident of the marbles took place later, when the buds, after swelling, began to burst with the sprouting of the young leaves. Everyone had begun to play marbles during recess, and Louis had some in his pocket which he fingered but, most of the time, dared not take out.

Most of them were fine-veined agates. Others had multicolored spirals inside the glass. He had not bought them. Vladimir, who now affected a protective air with him, had said one day, when he was feeling generous:

"You can take my marbles if you'd like. At my age, we no longer play kids' games."

Sometimes, however, Louis would take his marbles from his pocket in a corner of the yard and make them shine in the sun.

"Where did you buy them?"

He was being questioned by one of the big boys, a fellow named Randal, who regarded himself as the leader of the main group.

"I didn't buy them."

"You swiped them?"

Louis could feel that Randal was going to become menacing.

"I didn't. My big brother gave them to me."

"Well, you're going to give me the yellow one and the blue one."

"I won't."

"You're going to give me the yellow one and the blue one."

"I won't."

They were surrounded by four or five boys in Randal's gang.

"Did you hear what I said?"

"Yes, I did."

"You know what's going to happen?"

"No."

The big boy, who was a head taller than Louis, winked at his friends and then dashed at him. With an instinctive movement of defense, Louis, who was squeezing the marbles, thrust his fist into his trouser pocket, and Randal twisted his arm to make him pull out his hand.

"And now?"

"No."

They had rolled on the ground among the spectators' legs.

Randal punched and pulled and pushed. There was a ripping sound. The trousers, though they were of thick corduroy, had torn.

"You still refuse?"

"I do. They belong to me."

"They don't. You stole them."

One of the corners of Louis's lips was bleeding. Long black legs approached.

"What's going on here? Are you fighting?"

Randal sprang to his feet.

"No, sir. It's him."

"You mean that Cuchas attacked you?"

Louis stood up too and, running his hand over his lips, drew it away spotted with blood.

"Why were the two of you fighting?"

"We weren't fighting. He stole two of my marbles, a yellow one and a blue one, and won't give them back to me."

M. Charles studied the faces around him. The spectators said nothing. One or two of them, however, friends of Randal, nodded their heads affirmatively.

"Is it true, Cuchas?"

Then Louis, instead of answering, took his hand out of his

pocket, opened his fist, chose the two marbles that Randal had been hankering for, and handed them to his opponent. Randal was dumfounded. He hesitated to take them. Was M. Charles being taken in?

"Well, Randal, don't you want them any more?"

"I do, sir."

"You see, there was no need to tear your classmate's trousers and scratch his face."

"I apologize, sir."

But everyone could see that Cuchas was smiling, with a smile that was barely perceptible, like the reflection of an inner joy.

"Don't let it happen again. If I catch anyone fighting, he'll stay in for two hours."

From that day on, the evolution took place more rapidly, though it was barely visible, both among the students and in Louis's innermost heart.

Anyone could kick him as he went by without his hitting back or complaining to the teacher. When, on rare occasions, he brought a roll with a chocolate filling to eat during recess, all one had to do was demand it in a certain way and he would give it.

After school, almost all the others would leave in small groups, while he would walk off alone, with his school bag on his back, to the corner of Rue Mouffetard, looking at the house fronts, the sun or rain on the roofs, anything at all.

His smile was perhaps not a true smile but the reflection of a quiet and almost continuous satisfaction that could have been taken for placidness. Vladimir was not the only one who was irritated by this placidness. Smaller boys than Randal would attack Louis for the pleasure of feeling stronger than someone else.

"I bet if I slapped you, you wouldn't dare hit me back."

What could he have answered? He took the blow, didn't cry, and even disdained to put his hand to his cheek.

46

"You don't happen to have a screw loose, do you? Maybe you're a little batty, huh?"

"It's not only that he's batty. Don't you realize he takes himself for a little saint? I bet he goes to mass every Sunday. Maybe he's a choirboy."

He had never been to mass. Their mother never spoke to them about God except to exclaim, when a misfortune occurred:

"What have I done to that damned God?"

She had nevertheless married Heurteau in church, and there had been prayers of intercession for the dead before Emilie's body was taken to the cemetery.

Nor did he attend the course in religion which a vicar came to give once a week after school.

"No!" she had yelled when he had brought home from school the note asking parents whether or not they wished their child to receive religious education. "So he can talk to you about sin and make you start thinking I'm a bad woman! Religion's for the rich."

The little saint. The expression had been tossed off during a recreation period and was to stick to him all his life.

"Come here, little saint . . . You wouldn't happen to have a top in your pocket?"

For marble time was followed by top time. The chestnut trees were in bloom. They became fuller, with dark holes in their leaves. M. Charles always observed Louis with amazement, and at the end of the school year Louis was surprised to learn that he was at the head of his class.

He did not have the impression of having studied. He was embarrassed by the mocking or envious way his classmates looked at him.

On his way home, as he threaded his way through the crowd on Rue Mouffetard, the voice of a boy who was running and whom he did not have time to recognize cried out to him:

"Beat it, little saint!"

He was not a saint. If he did not swipe things, like Vladimir, it was not out of honesty but because he felt no desire to, or perhaps lacked courage. Too many people might start chasing him, people who ran faster and were stronger than he. He would be taken to the police station, then to prison.

For a time, he was afraid that Vladimir would be locked up. It was after vacation and during the winter, which was so cold that his mother and the other peddlers were obliged to light a charcoal burner near their pushcarts and keep warming their fingers which stuck out of their mittens.

One morning, when they were all in the kitchen sitting around the table, which was covered with oilcloth, someone knocked at the door. That was a bad sign, for the postman never went up to their apartment and nobody came to see them.

"Go open the door, Vladimir."

He had to go through the room, since the kitchen did not open on the corridor. Vladimir's mouth was full. They heard him turn the knob.

"Does Mme. Heurteau live here?"

The odd thing was that Vladimir, who was usually free with his tongue, did not say a word, and when he appeared in the doorway his face was livid with fear, his features were drawn, he had a shifty expression. Behind him they could see the uniform of a policeman with a weather-beaten face.

"Is your name Heurteau?"

He laboriously drew a piece of paper from his pocket. His hands were stiff with cold.

"Gabrielle Françoise Joséphine Heurteau, maiden name Cuchas . . ."

She was upset too, but not frightened, as Vladimir was.

"If you're from the neighborhood, you must be new, because I've never seen you. The other policemen can tell you that my license is in order, that I've never tampered with my weights or my scale, and that it's not like me to cause a disturbance in public."

Whereupon she grabbed her bowl of coffee and began to drink.

"When did you last see your husband?"

She did not act dumfounded. She really was dumfounded by that sudden mention of her former husband.

"Lambert?"

He looked at his paper again.

"Lambert Xavier Marie Heurteau, born at Saint-Josephère, Nièvre, on . . ."

What struck Louis most was that one of the given names of the twins' father was Marie.

"Wait, let me figure it out. Louis's going on eight. Eight or seven?"

She counted on her fingers.

"He'll be eight next September. The twins are ten. Lambert up and left one day between the two deliveries, ten or eleven months before Louis was born, so that I even wondered for a moment whether he wasn't his. How about a cup of coffee to warm you up?"

That permitted her to stand up, go to the closet for a bowl, and take the coffeepot from the stove.

"Have a seat."

There were only enough chairs for the members of the family, but Vladimir remained standing, distrustfully.

"You can see it was ages ago. Two lumps of sugar? Milk? To get back to Lambert, what's it all about?"

"Haven't you ever seen him again?"

"Never. Disappeared. Went off without leaving a trace, except debts in the saloons which I had to pay. That seems to be the law."

"He hasn't written to you?"

"In the first place, he wouldn't have been able to write. He could hardly sign his name."

"It says here that he was a tilesetter by trade."

"When he felt like working. I'd say that he was a loafer by

trade. He'd hardly be on a job a week and right away he'd injure his hand or foot or get bronchitis—when he didn't argue with the foreman. Bear in mind, I don't hold it against him. He had a weak chest and he used to spit blood. Once a month he went for a checkup to Cochin Hospital where they made them line up in the yard in the middle of winter. They told him he had to build himself up, that the climate was bad for him, that it would be better if he lived near Nice. Can you see us at Nice? So he didn't believe them. The first thing he'd do when he left the hospital was to go to a saloon. When he came back, he was blind drunk and couldn't take his pants off."

"Did you argue?"

"Just look at me. Do I look like a woman who argues with people? Ask anyone in the whole street if Gabrielle ever argued in her life! Even with the grouchiest customers, I tell them what I think of them with a smile. He beat me occasionally, but I didn't defend myself, because it didn't hurt."

"I have orders to take you with me."

"To the police station?"

"To the morgue. Some of the bums on Place Maubert have recognized him, but since according to the record you're still his wife, you've got to come and recognize him officially."

"Lambert's dead?"

She did not speak in a tragic voice. She was barely astonished, without any sadness.

"Did they finally put him in a hospital? I'm idiotic! If he died in a hospital, you wouldn't be taking me to the morgue, would you? Well, well! Children, who'd have expected such news when I lit the fire this morning? . . ."

The twins continued indifferently to eat their thick slices of bread and butter which they dipped into coffee and milk. It was about a father they had hardly known. Perhaps Alice remembered his face, his mustache which used to smell of wine or brandy.

Had he ever bounced them up and down on his knees or held their hands and taken them for a walk in the empty streets on Sunday? Did Heurteau even have a Sunday suit?

Alice was particularly interested in the young policeman's ruddy face, and Louis was fascinated by the silver buttons of his tunic, which he was seeing at such close range for the first time and which he would have liked to touch.

"As a matter of fact, how did he die?"

"He threw himself into the Seine from the Pont Marie at about eleven at night. Some tramps who had made a fire under the bridge and who knew him went to inform the river police, but it wasn't till two hours later that they fished out the body more than a half mile downstream. The only thing they found in his pockets was an old dirty military-service certificate."

"Since we've got to go, let's get going."

She was looking for her shawl and mittens. Alice asked, in the hollow voice she had got into the habit of assuming whenever she knew in advance that the answer would be no:

"Can I go with you?"

She was quite unmoved. Her face merely looked longer, her features sharper, and her nostrils more pinched. Her mother gave her a look that Louis had rarely seen in her eyes.

"Are you depraved or something? So now you feel like taking a squint at a stiff?"

He did not attend the funeral. He did not even know whether there was an actual funeral, a ceremony in church, a procession, a coffin that was lowered into the grave with ropes, in a cemetery.

He had once followed a hearse, out of curiosity, to know what it was like. He admired hearses, especially those of second-class funerals, with tassels and silver fringes, with horses attired in a kind of cloak.

He was also impressed by the women who were hardly recognizable behind their crepe veils and who held a handkerchief in their hand. The cemetery was beautiful. It was pleasant to walk in the lanes covered with dead leaves that made an odd sound beneath the soles of his shoes.

In any case, if they had been Catholics he would have liked to be the choirboy in a white surplice who walked in front of everybody and held a long black pole surmounted with a crucifix.

Heurteau was a pauper, a word Louis had often heard but the meaning of which he had only recently learned. Somewhere in the fabulous neighborhood through which the coachman had driven them one Sunday lived the rich people who, for him, belonged to another species and whom one was not likely to meet on Rue Mouffetard. Then came the bourgeois, about whom his mother sometimes spoke and who were located, in his mind, on wide, quiet streets and on avenues, such as Avenue des Gobelins or Boulevard du Port-Royal where they lived in gray stone houses.

There were also the landlords, for example those opposite, above M. Stieb's store, who did nothing but collect rent and evict tenants who didn't pay.

The storekeepers, both the important ones and the less important, lived apart. Last came the mass of the poor, the majority of the people who lived on the street and in the neighborhood.

The paupers did not have enough to eat every day. When they were sick, they were visited by persons from Public Assistance who gave them bread tickets so that they would not actually die, and some of them, when they were drunk, slept on the sidewalk with old newspapers under their jackets instead of blankets.

Heurteau was a pauper, like the tenants at the back of the yard, like the one whom people had seen from their windows with a knife in his belly.

"What do they do with paupers when they die?"

"They're buried in the paupers' grave. Or else, if nobody claims them, M. Kob attends to them."

Had his mother claimed Heurteau? He wasn't sure. He dared not ask her. He preferred to imagine M. Kob cutting him up on a big table and carefully laying out the pieces, as on the butcher's counter.

Gabrielle was receiving male visitors again. In fact, there were always such visitors, except during the weeks following Emilie's death. Their absence had been their mother's way of being in mourning.

She also spent a few nights alone after the death of her husband, about whom there had never been much talk in the family but who thereafter was never mentioned again. Nevertheless, the wedding photo in its black and gold frame remained in its place on the wall of the room.

Louis was beginning to be aware of his physical appearance. There was a mirror in a store window that was full of hats with flowers on them, and he would sometimes look at himself in it. He was really short, much shorter than boys of his age, but his features were very fine. They were not the features of a baby or a little boy but already those of a man, and his bright eyes sparkled. His lips were more curved than those of his brothers and even of his sister. He blushed easily, especially when a passer-by, male or female, caught sight of him observing himself in the mirror. And yet he was not vain. Perhaps, had he been able to transform himself, he would have preferred to be a big, rough, jeering fellow like Vladimir. The day he received his report card, he had merely put it on the kitchen table, without saying anything, and forty-eight hours went by before his mother happened to open it and learn that he was at the head of his class.

"So," she exclaimed in amazement, "you're the most intelligent of the lot! It's the first time anyone in the family got first prize."

Whereupon Vladimir had snapped bitterly and mockingly:

"He's the little saint!"

"What do you mean?"

"That's what his classmates call him. Because he lets himself get knocked around without defending himself. All he does is put up his arms to protect himself, and then he refuses to tell the teacher who hit him."

"Is that true, Louis?"

"I'm the smallest."

He was lying, and the proof was that his cheeks turned pink. Even if he had been built like the twins, he probably would not have hit back. The blows didn't hurt much. After a few seconds, he didn't feel anything and there was no point getting involved in a fight. Someday they would tire of always picking on the same one and would let him daydream in his corner.

He didn't like people to bother about him, didn't like to be asked questions, to be torn from his thoughts of the moment. He had always been interested in the stove, the stairway, the yard, the carpenter's shop, the stalls in the street, but he was now becoming interested in people too, in his mother, in his brothers, in the faces he saw in the street. However, even with regard to his family he felt untouched, he remained apart, without suffering or rejoicing at anything whatever.

"M. Pliska, a friend of mine."

Their mother sometimes introduced those of her lovers who spent several nights or several weeks with them. They occasionally played with the children.

M. Pliska, whom she called Stefan, lasted at least two months, which included the period of the Christmas vacation. He was a big fellow of not more than twenty-five, with a powerful build. When he stood in the kitchen, the room seemed too small for him, and the chairs creaked under his weight.

They did not know what he did for a living. When Gabrielle got up to go to Les Halles, he would stretch out on the bed and sleep late, until nine or ten o'clock. The noise did not waken him.

He was very fair, in fact his hair was almost white, and he had orange-colored skin that was pitted in spots with smallpox marks. He spoke only a few words of French but tried to understand what was said. Without taking an interest in Vladimir or the twins, he had immediately singled out Louis, though he often paid compliments to Alice, whom he pretended to treat as a young lady. He even kissed her hand at times, though there was no telling whether he was being playful or serious.

"Pretty!" He would go into raptures. "Much pretty!"

Nothing could prevent him from going down to the yard bare-chested, wearing only underpants and an overcoat thrown over his shoulders, and washing himself thoroughly at the faucet. When he came up again, he glowed with satisfaction and would hum a Czech song, prepare his shaving brush and sharpen his razor, for he wore neither beard nor mustache.

"It's what?" he asked Louis, pointing to the only mirror in the apartment.

"A mirror."

"Mir-ro-ar . . .," he repeated painstakingly.

"Or a glass."

"Glass? Why glass? Me drink from glass . . ."

Although he did not mind the cold, he nonetheless appreciated the pleasant warmth of the stove, near which he would sit with a pocket chess set on his knees.

"How you say . . . ?"

Those were his favorite words: How you say?

He outlined a crown on his head with his finger. "Queen, yes? . . . Queen will take castle . . ."

It was so entrancing, thanks to his mimicry, that within two weeks Louis knew the chessmen, how they functioned, and a few of the standard moves.

"You play? Me give you queen and castles . . ."

It was the only Christmas that the family really celebrated. Other years, they contented themselves with eating forcemeat sausage. On the evening of December 24th, M. Pliska returned with a three-foot Christmas tree which he set up in the middle of the table, and then placed packages on it: a jellied chicken, meat pie, ham, and a bottle of sparkling wine.

For Gabrielle he had bought an enameled brooch in the shape of a rose, for Vladimir a whistle that resembled a police whistle, for Alice a thimble which was so light that a needle would probably go through it. It was the intention that counted. The twins each received a top and Louis a box of colored pencils.

Everyone could have some of the wine, and when he saw that the bottle was almost empty he rushed out in his shirt sleeves and came back a minute later with a second bottle and a bag of cookies.

Then he sang, and after that he insisted that Gabrielle sing too.

"She's woman of my life!" he cried in a burst of enthusiasm, turning to the children after she had sung a ballad of which she remembered only the first stanza and the end of the last.

The street was bright and noisy. The shops were all open, and all the windows were lit up. It was like a canal of light, and Louis went to the window several times to look out, for he was no longer hungry for the cookies, and the sparkling wine had made him feel a little nauseous.

M. Pliska's ideas always occurred to him abruptly. Suddenly he would stand up and dash to the corridor as if seized with an urgent need. This time he stayed out longer, so long that when he returned, triumphantly, the children were undressed. He brandished in triumph, while repeating a Czech word, a square bottle covered with unreadable signs and containing a yellowish liquor.

"For Christmas! . . . Only Christmas! . . . Health, woman my life . . . My life always . . ."

Gabrielle sipped it warily and remarked that it was strong, but she must have got used to it, for she remained in the kitchen part of the night drinking it. The children, who were over-excited, slept badly. At times they were awakened by M. Pliska's singing, at times by his sobs, and finally by the clang of the bedsprings on which he and Gabrielle collapsed.

He usually disappeared in the afternoon and was away for part of the evening too.

"Me work . . . Much work . . ."

He would point to his head in order to explain that it was with his brain that he worked. He would also sulk at times, would not say a word for two days, except to explain to Louis, who was definitely his favorite:

"Mother cruel . . . All women cruel . . . Men very unhappy . . . Pliska unhappy . . ."

He had brought an odd-shaped valise, with railroad labels pasted on it, which remained for a long time in the corner of the room where Emilie's cot had been and in which he carefully arranged his clothes and other personal effects.

What, indeed, had become of the cot? It had disappeared almost at the same time as the little girl. No doubt it had ended up in a secondhand store.

Pliska in turn disappeared, as did his valise. Gabrielle did not explain why. She never explained. Perhaps she did not try to explain the whys and wherefores of things even to herself.

For Louis, it was the winter of discoveries. The first of these hardly surprised him. One night when he had awakened with a start from a bad dream and the moon had kept him from falling asleep again, he had gone to the window and leaned against it quietly with his elbows. The big moon lit up the landscape more brightly than the lamppost and made it look unreal. Four garbage cans, so full that the lids did not close, were lined up on the sidewalk just in front of the alley.

He had often seen ragpickers poking about in garbage cans with their spiked sticks and thrusting whatever was still usable into the bag they carried on their back or into a baby carriage.

That night, two people were rummaging in the garbage cans opposite, a man and a woman, but they were not ragpickers, and what they were looking for was crusts of bread, anything edible, which they immediately stuffed into their mouths.

They were not old. They were not wearing rags, like the tramps of Place Maubert. They were younger than the children's mother, a bit older than M. Pliska. So there existed a category below the paupers who received bread tickets or help from Public Assistance or who could get a bowl of soup at the Salvation Army. When they had finished going through the four cans, they started walking down the street. Without a word, without looking at each other.

The second discovery was more important. To begin with, he knew that Vladimir's friend, the Spaniards' son, was called Ramon, for when he passed the shop one day he heard the boy's mother call him by name before yelling to him something that Louis did not understand.

Two or three times, while walking in the street after four o'clock, when the lights went on, he had noticed his brother and Ramon strolling along with a self-assumed air of animals on the alert. Not only was Vladimir the taller and more resolute of the two, but Louis could feel that he was the leader and that his companion was his slave.

It must have been a Saturday night, for there were more people than usual in the narrow street which was narrowed even more by the stands that overflowed the stores and by the carts of the peddlers.

Louis had just spoken to his mother. He was on his way home when he saw Vladimir and Ramon standing on the curb. They were talking in a low voice, with an expression of self-importance. Vladimir really looked like a leader, and even from a distance Louis could tell that he was giving an order.

Ramon, who was wearing a blue frieze overcoat with gilt

buttons, was hesitating and making objections, and finally Vladimir simply shoved him off the sidewalk by poking him in the side with his knee.

Once again, in the middle of the street, Ramon turned around imploringly but encountered only the hard look on his friend's face. In front of him was a butcher shop that specialized in poultry and game. A wild boar, which was partly cut up, was hanging from a hook near a garland of wild ducks and other birds that were unfamiliar to Louis, who had never seen them alive or eaten them.

On a stall lay plucked chickens that were marked with a label and, to the left of the door, unskinned wild rabbits.

Two women were waiting their turn. An old gentleman in a bowler hat was being shown some birds at which he kept sniffing.

Ramon waited for the moment when no one was looking in his direction, grabbed a rabbit, slipped it under his coat and started walking very fast while Vladimir, on the other sidewalk, ambled up the street.

Louis followed them with his eyes. They got together on the dimly lit Rue de l'Arbalète, where Ramon handed his friend the rabbit as if performing an act of homage or offering his tribute of loyalty.

Vladimir took it by the ears, swung it around two or three times and tossed it into the first alley they came to.

Louis then remembered the watch, candy, and miscellaneous objects that his brother used to hide in his mattress. Did he still collect them? Louis had never since been curious enough to find out. He didn't care. The important thing was that Vladimir had been able to make Ramon steal. Was it actually the Spaniard who had swiped the watch? Probably not. He seemed to be a novice. He had implored Vladimir and had crossed the street reluctantly.

A rabbit that was good to eat was now lying in an alley where rats would soon be squabbling over it.

Louis said nothing about the matter to anyone. He never said anything.

One day he saw a gathering at the head of the street and had no difficulty worming his way up front. It was simply a crowd of onlookers surrounding a pitchman, a tall, bony, lantern-jawed fellow with an enormous nose who was contorting his face as if it were made of rubber.

"Now listen closely, ladies and gentlemen, and if the ladies are wise and their husbands have common sense, every family is going to gain a quarter of an hour a day, to say nothing of avoiding three or four fights every week."

He was not wearing a detachable collar. From a small valise, which he barely opened, as if it contained treasures, he took a very high collar with a double lining and, looking as if he were squirming in front of a mirror, attached it with two buttons.

"First and easiest operation, especially if your wife or girl friend lends a hand."

Another dip into the suitcase, from which this time he withdrew an aggressively purple tie.

"And now for the second morning operation to which elegant men are condemned. Bear in mind that this tie is new and therefore easier to handle than an old one."

Then followed a comedy which he played with his hands, eyes, neck, mouth, in fact with his whole body, twisting and turning in order to work the tie up between the two plies of the starched collar.

After which, he gave up in exhaustion, wiped his forehead, and beckoned to a plump, jovial woman in the audience who had a shopping bag under her arm.

"So you, Madame, are willing to be my spouse for a moment. You've nothing to be afraid of. We're in public and I know how to behave. Be so good as to help me get this tie on."

He had taken her shopping bag and slipped the tie into her pudgy fingers. As she was shorter than he, he leaned forward comically, acting as if he were half strangled each time she raised the flap of the collar.

"And *that,* ladies and gentlemen, is the cause of half—what am I saying?—of three quarters of family fights, the other quarter being caused by our better half's corset. Unfortunately I don't go in for corsets because police headquarters forbids such demonstrations in public."

All that remained for him to do was to take from the valise a celluloid device to which the tie was attached in the twinkling of an eye. Two or three seconds later, it was set in the collar.

"Ladies and gentlemen, unfortunately not everybody will be able to take advantage of this work of genius which will ensure peace in the family and put valets out of work."

The valise was finally opened. Just as the sale was beginning, one of the spectators nudged his wife with his elbow and, pointing to Louis, who was still up front, whispered:

"I've never seen such a shrewd look as on that child's face!"

Louis heard him and did not smile. He already knew, in a vague kind of way, that it was not true, that he was not shrewd at all, that he had simply been watching and taking in the spectacle and that every detail of the scene, the peddler's twisted mouth, the dumpy woman's black polka-dot dress, the wart on her cheek, the expression of the various spectators, was inside him.

He was not laughing at them. He did not think them ridiculous. He had never yet thought anything ridiculous or seen anything not worth watching with interest.

IV

VLADIMIR HAD STOPPED going to school. He had not succeeded in getting his diploma. Or rather, no doubt, though he did not bother to explain to anyone—except perhaps to Ramon—he had not wanted to get it, out of protest, out of defiance.

From the very beginning, he had made a point of being at the bottom of the class. He had always been big for his age, and at about fifteen he had suddenly grown almost four inches.

Not only were his clothes tight on him, but he was not used to his height and his movements were awkward. His gait was at times too manly and at times too childish. His face was covered with a dark fuzz that made him look unwashed, and Louis once caught him putting their mother's powder on his face to cover his pimples.

For two or three weeks, he had almost never been seen during the day. He did not wander along Rue Mouffetard with his Spanish friend, who was now at a *lycée,* where he wore the school uniform. What did Vladimir do with his days? He would come home at night looking, at one and the same time, feverish, arrogant, and depressed.

"When are you going to make up your mind to work?" his mother would ask him.

He would answer like a man who was not obliged to account for what he does:

"You'll see."

She was definitely worried when she saw him wearing a new suit for which she had not given him money, new shoes, a white shirt, and a wing collar.

"Starting Monday morning, I'll be working for M. Brillanceau as an apprentice."

"The locksmith on Rue Tournefort? You want to become a locksmith?"

He had reached his decision alone and had not discussed the matter with anyone, and nobody ever knew by what process or after what experiences he had come to choose the locksmith's trade.

Louis knew the shop, which was not far from his school. It was at the corner of an alley, of which there were many in the neighborhood, on the side of the street that did not get the sun, and the windows were so dirty, the walls so dark, with hundreds of keys and tools hanging from nails, that a gas lamp burned all day long.

M. Brillanceau had the color of his trade. He was gray and sad-eyed. A curved pipe, most of the time unlit, was always in his mouth, as if it had been dug into his grisly mustache.

Vladimir started work at seven in the morning. He took with him a canteen of coffee and slices of bread and butter in an old biscuit can.

Life at home suddenly began to change quickly. Alice was thirteen and, though she was frail, looked older than she was. She had barely passed the examination for her diploma, but refused to continue her studies and stayed at home, where she did the housework and prepared the meals.

"What did you do when you were my age?"

To which Gabrielle replied frankly:

"I'd rather not tell you."

At times, Alice would replace her mother at the pushcart for an hour. At times too, in the evening, she would disappear for a rather long time, and when she undressed before lying down on the mattress next to his, Louis would get a whiff of an odor foreign to the family, an odor of boy.

She was pale, but pretty enough for people to turn around to look at her as she went by. She was beginning to put on make-up, but ineptly, which gave her a dubious look. With her small pear-shaped breasts and the sparse, blonde down between her thighs, she would strut about nude in front of her brothers, dragging her clothes.

There was a feeling in the air that things were starting to go to pieces. There was no longer the old solidarity in the home, and one night there was a violent scene during which Louis saw his mother in a rage for the first time.

For the past few days she had been coming home with a middle-aged man she called Papa who spent the night with her behind the torn curtain. He was a huge, hairy-chested fellow with impressive hands. He probably worked at Les Halles, for he left with her in the morning, without bothering to wash his face. He had a strong smell and made love very fast, with strong thrusts that shook the floor, after which he crashed down on the bed and sank into sleep.

One night, the fourth or the fifth, Louis was awakened by Gabrielle's shrill voice.

"Let go of her, you son of a bitch!"

It was still dark. The sky was just beginning to turn grayish, vaguely lighting up the room, as did the gaslight from the lamppost. Louis, without moving, half opened his eyes and saw the man's bulk on the bed of his sister, of whom all that was visible was her blonde hair.

"Let her alone, you hear, you pig?"

He kept breathing hard and emitting a kind of laugh. Perhaps Gabrielle and he had been drinking the night before, as she so often did with others.

She tried to pull him off the mattress.

"Get the hell away, you whore!"

Vladimir, who suddenly awoke, punched him on the back of his head with both fists, but the man didn't seem to feel anything. Then Gabrielle, who was in her shirt, ran into the kitchen, came back with the poker and started beating him with it, screaming with all her might:

"You bastard! You pig! You sex maniac!"

He began to groan and got down on all fours with a dazed look, uncovering the body of Alice, who put her hands to her face.

Gabrielle kept hitting him, and blood spurted at the base of his skull, while he staggered painfully to his feet.

The twins, who had not stirred, were surely awake. The scene wavered between the grotesque and the tragic. All the protagonists were in their shirts. For some reason or other, perhaps out of habit, the man had kept his socks on.

He looked like an ox that the killer in the abattoir had failed to knock out with his cleaver. Louis would have sworn, later, that the man's eyes had become red. He stood there with his huge hands open, hesitating to dash at Gabrielle, who was still holding the poker and standing up to him.

"Mama!" screamed one of the twins with terror as the man took a step toward her.

"Don't you worry about me! I'll attend to him!"

The poker rose and came down hard. Luckily it missed his head, grazed his cheek, and landed on his shoulder. There was a sound as of a bone cracking.

"And now, you swine, if you haven't had enough, say so!"

She turned around without hesitating, fearing nothing more from him, picked up the clothes that were piled on the floor, walked to the door and threw them into the corridor.

"Get the hell out if you don't want me to finish you, you dirty rat!"

Then the big shoes were sent flying into the narrow hallway toward which the man she had called Papa a few hours earlier was staggering.

Heedless of the neighbors, she slammed the door in his face and when she came back she was still so excited that she knocked over the chamber pot.

Standing in the middle of the room, she yelled at her daughter, who was hiding her face.

"And you, couldn't you scream, you little bitch? Admit you liked it!"

One shitty business, as Gabrielle would say with her fondness for expressive words, brings another. The following day, a letter arrived, something that almost never happened. The principal of the school "requested Mme. Heurteau to be so good as to come to his office regarding an important matter."

Louis was expecting it. For some weeks he had been seeing the redheads less and less often at recess. They left and returned with their school bags at the usual time, but they did not go to school.

When Gabrielle got home, she was furious, though this time her fury was partly an act.

"You, the two of you, so you imagine I've got it too easy and you've got to complicate my life, is that it? I want to know where you go traipsing most days? You, Guy, answer me."

He was the more vulnerable of the two, and though they were born the same day he looked younger than his brother.

"I don't know, Mama."

"You don't know how you spend your time?"

Her hand became menacing and Olivier spoke up.

"We don't like school, Mama. They've got it in for us. We're blamed for everything. When someone talks in class, the teacher doesn't try to find out who it was. He says, 'Redheads, be quiet!'

He doesn't call us by our names, like the other boys. We're 'the redheads.' And we're always the ones, even when we haven't done anything, who have to stand in the corner. The kids keep away from us and claim we smell of rotten vegetables."

"Who said that?"

"All of them. They're all against us."

Because of the vegetables, solidarity was springing up again.

"Didn't you ask them what their mothers do?"

"No, Mama, we didn't."

That was the twins' shrewd side.

"Some of them are in a dirtier trade than me and I know at least two who earn their living with their behinds. You can tell them that next time. But you've got to go to school, because it seems they've done some investigating, that I'm not a good mother, that I let you bum around and don't look after you. The pompous idiot I went to see who they call the principal threatened to send a report to the police asking that you be sent to an institution."

"An institution?"

"I think that's the word he used. He meant a reformatory!"

Was there any connection between those events and the habit that Louis began to fall into shortly thereafter of accompanying his mother to Les Halles? He did not ask himself the question. As with many of his ways and acts which were to stand out in his memory, it simply happened one day, without his trying to know why.

One spring morning, very early, before sunrise, while his mother was dressing, he asked her in a humble tone as he lay on his mattress:

"Can I come with you?"

"To Les Halles?"

"That's right. I've felt like doing it for a long time."

"You need sleep."

"I won't fall asleep again anyway. Once, Mama! Just once!"

He was not faking. His intention was to go with his mother just once.

He had already slipped on his trousers and he dressed more quickly than ever. Except in winter, when she lit the fire before leaving, their mother did not drink her coffee at home.

"Are you the one who's going to push the cart?" she joked as they went down the dark stairway where they had to run their hands along the wall so as not to miss a step.

"I'll try."

It was an exciting experience. In the yard, he already smelled the odor of night, which is not the same as that of day, and he was surprised, as they walked up the street, to see a light. It lit up a narrow, shallow saloon in which two dark tables stood near the horseshoe-shaped bar. The bald saloonkeeper was wearing a very white shirt, the sleeves of which were rolled up, and a blue apron.

A woman with a shawl over her shoulders was leaning on the bar with her elbow and dipping her croissant into a cup of coffee and milk. It was a new smell, a new image too, and Louis was happy at the thought that almost everybody was still asleep at that hour.

"Hello, Céline! Ernest, two javas."

He placed two glasses, first one and then the other, under the percolator, which let out a jet of steam.

"With milk for the kid?"

"Do you want milk, Louis?"

"A little. Can I have a croissant?"

There was a basketful of them. They had just come out of the oven and were still warm and crisp, and he was allowed to eat four of them, which had never happened in his life.

The boss turned to a shelf and grabbed a bottle at the end of which was a long tin nozzle, and without asking, no doubt following a daily rite, he tossed a dash of liquor into the mother's coffee, which immediately gave off a different smell.

68

She too was eating croissants. She ordered a second cup, which received another dash.

"You on your way, Gabrielle? Did you sell out yesterday?"

"There was just about enough left to make soup with."

Everything was different, the sound of footsteps on the sidewalk, the way the houses looked. Some were four stories high, two or three with red brick fronts; another, which was painted white, adjoined houses that were only one story high. An empty hack went by with the coachman dozing on the seat.

They turned right at Rue du Pot-de-Fer and entered a yard where they joined other women, among whom was the grandmother. A sleepy little man with a potbelly was in charge. Each of the women picked one of the pushcarts lined up against a wall and then went to get her scale and weights in a dark shed.

"Where'd you spend the night, Henriette?"

They yelled to each other, laughed like little girls during recess, joshed each other, exchanged catty remarks that only they could understand. Some were young and some were old. Most of them were big women with blotchy faces, pudgy fingers, and swollen ankles.

Without waiting, they left the yard and went down Rue Lhomond. When they passed the Pantheon, the sky was getting lighter, and on Boulevard Saint-Michel an omnibus drawn by six horses with clopping shoes almost hit the pushcart as it went by.

"You and your hearse!" yelled his mother.

They crossed the Pont Saint-Michel, and Louis, who stayed at the right because Gabrielle wanted him to be nearer the sidewalk, pushed with all his might. He would have liked to be between the shafts and roll the cart by himself, but he dared not ask his mother to let him.

The Courthouse was dark and empty and only a yellowish-green light shone above the gate of the morgue.

After the Pont au Change the streets began to get lively. Several omnibuses were waiting to leave. Then, on Rue des Halles, there were all kinds of noises. He saw carts that were loaded with pyramids of cabbages and carrots, crates full of live chickens and rabbits.

The people there were wide-awake, because activity had started long before, for many of them even before midnight, and beyond the gaslit warehouses, from which issued an unbroken din, a continuous stamping and trampling, yells, calls, oaths, and laughter, stood a little train of cars behind its locomotive, which was puffing peacefully.

"Do your feet hurt?"

"No, Mama."

"Aren't you cold?"

His feet didn't hurt, he wasn't cold, and he was having the greatest adventure of his life. His nostrils quivered without managing to take in all the smells, for they changed every ten yards.

There were vegetables, fruit, poultry, cases of eggs, everywhere, on the sidewalks, in the gutter, all over the storehouses, and everything was moving, was heaped in one place and then transported to another.

Figures were yelled. People were writing in black pads with violet pencils. Market porters wearing big hats and carrying a side of beef on their shoulder rushed through the streets. Tubs were overflowing with guts. Women sitting on stools were plucking poultry with the rapidity of magicians.

It all looked chaotic, but he would soon learn that, for all the apparent disorder, every wagon, every crate, every cauliflower, every rabbit, every man had a definite place and precise job.

He saw there people of a kind who hung around Rue Mouffetard, bearded old men in rags, with long hair down to the back of their neck, who were carrying crates that were too heavy for them from a wagon to a warehouse while a young man jotted down a check beside their name each time they entered.

The grandmother went by, and Gabrielle yelled out to her: "It's a good day for red cabbage."

Why? He realized that she had seen everything, the price marks on piles of merchandise, the vegetables that other peddlers of Rue Mouffetard were already loading on their carts.

"Got to be shrewd in our line of work," she explained to Louis.

He was grateful to her for saying this, for it was the first time she had ever spoken to him in confidence about her professional life.

"Some women buy anything just because it's cheap."

She would listen to figures that were quoted as she went by. She stopped, tempted, in front of some crates of potatoes.

"How much?"

Then, without answering, she continued pushing her cart toward a street where the bustle continued, and entered a high-ceilinged shed. On a blackboard, next to the names of foods, were figures written in chalk which a man in a black smock kept changing constantly, the way the teacher did on the dais.

Clerks were working in a glass-enclosed cage. Everything went fast. You had to have your wits about you not to be knocked over by one of the porters, and Louis instinctively held on to an end of his mother's apron.

"Have you got any red cabbage, Samuel?"

"Did you see it on the board?"

"It's not there."

"Go ask François. There may be a few crates left."

She did not change her mind easily, and Louis was pleased to see that everyone knew her and treated her with affectionate familiarity. She got her red cabbage and they started going back, but by other streets in order to avoid those that were too crowded to get through easily.

The sun was up. The windows of the houses were shining. The blues were bluer, the pinks pinker, the reds redder. He began to see cooks and even well-dressed women carrying shopping bags.

They passed three men in evening clothes and top hats coming out of a restaurant in the company of young women covered with frills and furbelows. One of the men who was a little the worse for drink wanted to hire a marketer's horse and wagon at any price in order to drive home.

Louis was pushing with all his might. He felt the resistance of every paving stone. His mother stopped before the Châtelet.

"Wait for me here."

She entered a wineshop where she was served a small glass as a matter of course. She tossed down her drink, took a coin from the moneybag under her apron, and threw it on the bar. It was a glorious morning, bursting with life. Everything was alive. Everything was colorful. Everything smelled good and he drank the air rather than breathed it.

"Aren't you tired?"

"Not at all, Mama!"

"What are you going to do till it's time to go to school?"

For at half past six she was already setting up her pushcart in its usual place, opposite the fish store, and she was not the first.

"Don't worry. I'll find something to do."

His head was spinning, his legs were limp, he was stuffed. He walked slowly up the dark stairway and opened the door of the room, where the twins were still sleeping. His sister was in the kitchen lighting wood for the coffee.

"Has Vladimir left?"

"Five minutes ago. Where have you been?"

"I went with Mama."

"To Les Halles? She let you? Are you hungry?"

"I ate croissants."

"Lucky you!"

He was tempted to stretch out on his mattress in order to digest in peace what he had just lived through. His cheeks were flushed, and he knew that if he let himself lie down he would sink into blissful slumber.

He made himself sit by the window and go over his homework. Alice went to wake the twins with little kicks, and they groaned before getting up. They were in their shirts. Their hair was sticking up and their eyes were bleary.

"Hey, little saint, what are you doing?"

"I'm not doing anything."

They were aggressive as soon as they awoke!

"He went to Les Halles with Mama."

"What for?"

"Ask him."

"Just to see," said Louis casually.

He did not yet know that it would become a routine or that in the classroom he would relish the torpor that kept him suspended between dream and reality.

"Are you dreaming, Cuchas?"

"No, sir."

"Twelve times twenty-seven?"

"Three hundred twenty-four."

A vague smile, which no one understood, would drift over his face.

The morning trip to the market behind his mother's pushcart was to play an important role in his memories and his life, but legends grew up around the experience and it became difficult, even for him, to distinguish clearly between truth, exaggeration, and falsehood.

People wrote, for example, that for several years, despite his age and weak constitution, he got up every night at three in the morning, winter and summer alike. But his mother did not always go out at three in the morning. It depended on the season. In the fall, she would leave Rue Mouffetard later, for there would have been no point in being at her post with her wares at six o'clock, when there was no one in the street and the lampposts were still lit.

There were also mornings when, depending on her companion, she would let herself sleep an extra hour or two.

In any case, Louis himself did not always wake up. It was true that often, as soon as his mother awoke, he did too, that he sometimes was up before her, but at times he would fall asleep again, unless it was a Thursday[1] or a holiday, or during vacation.

People also said that the women of Les Halles were so amazed to see a child impose such discipline on himself in order to help his mother that they had nicknamed him the little saint. In what way could he help her, in the beginning, he with his skinny arms? It was for his own sake that he went, in order to renew the wonder of it, to complete his set of exciting images, for example, that of the Seine, which had hardly struck him the first time, of the tugboats that pulled their barges and disappeared for a moment beneath the arch of the bridge, of the horse-drawn canal boats which a carter followed slowly along the towpath. He was constantly discovering images, yellow and green house fronts, signboards, nooks crowded with barrels.

It was not the women of the market but his schoolmates who had nicknamed him the little saint. The term had reached the market by chance. A woman with whom his mother was bargaining over baskets of plums on the sidewalk had gone into raptures in his presence.

"What a pretty child! He's like a miniature!"

Though he no longer had long hair like a girl, it was still longer than that of most boys and, being very fine, tended to

[1] French children do not go to school on Thursday, but do on Saturday. —Translator's note.

flutter about his face, which thereby seemed all the more delicately designed.

Gabrielle had replied:

"It would be better for him not to be a miniature but a brute like his brothers. The kids in school take advantage of his size and hit him, and since he won't tell who did it they call him the little saint."

It was also related that he had acquired a passion for chess at the age of six because M. Pliska had sat with him in front of the kitchen stove for a few days and shown him how the pieces moved.

But it was not until a year or two later, when he began to be given spending money for Sunday, that he saved up to buy a cheap pocket chess set, the pieces of which were made not of ivory or wood but cardboard.

When it rained, he would sometimes sit near the window bent over the black and white squares for an hour.

At about that time, the landlord, M. Doré, decided to install gas in the house, and the kerosene lamp, which was no longer needed because of the incandescent gas-mantles that hung not only in the middle of the kitchen but in the middle of the room as well, ended up in a secondhand store, like Emilie's cot.

The mantles, which were delicately suspended from the end of the gas tube, were made of a fragile material and turned to dust as soon as anyone touched them or when they were shaken. They gave rise to a whole series of minor dramas, for on the floor above lived an Italian family from Piedmont with seven or eight children.

The father, a construction worker, wore heavy boots and kept them on when he got home in the evening. He would walk up and down the room, play with the children, and make the ceiling tremble, with the result that the mantles in the room had to be changed twice a week.

"I'm going upstairs to those brutes and tell them a thing or two!"

Gabrielle would go bravely up the stairs, which were now lit by a gas burner with a dancing flame that was at times white and at times yellow. She would knock on the door, and for a quarter of an hour there would be an exchange of insults in French and Italian.

The children would cry, their mother would yelp. Vladimir, if he was at home, would go to the rescue.

Other tenants, disturbed by the noise, would yell at everyone, and once, when Louis had gone upstairs to see what was going on, he discovered through the chink of a door a skeleton-like, glassy-eyed old woman who already belonged to another world and who was telling her beads.

Had it not been for that incident, he would never have known she existed, for she never left her room and it was not until six or seven months later that she was taken away very early one morning, on the sly, in a white pine coffin that resembled the crates in the market.

Vladimir was still working for M. Brillanceau. He wore a cap and a pair of heavy blue overalls. He smoked cigarettes which he rolled and let droop from his lower lip in an affected way.

In the street, he walked with his hands in his pockets, rolling his shoulders with an air of disdain, as if everyone were watching him.

He was losing weight. His face was peaked and the rings under his eyes grew darker and darker. There were evenings when he did not get home until twelve o'clock, and one winter night, which Louis could not place exactly, he did not return until breakfast.

He had a new way of treating the men who spent the night with their mother. He would look them up and down mockingly and aggressively, as if challenging them to pick a fight with him.

One Sunday morning—it was still winter—a tall young man with the head of a musician was drinking his coffee and eating bread and butter with them when Vladimir, who almost always slept late on Sunday, entered the kitchen. His eyes were bleary.

"You're not satisfied with sleeping with my mother, but she has to support you as well."

He was obviously in a bad temper, ready for anything, ready to bite.

"Keep quiet, Vladimir, and mind your own business. Don't get up, Philippe. Don't mind what he says. He's always like that in the morning and an hour later he forgets all about it."

The musician nevertheless preferred to leave, and his departure took place amidst an awkward and painful silence. No sooner was the door closed than Vladimir attacked again. Pouring himself a bowl of coffee, he sat down, with his elbows on the table, and snapped at his mother:

"Do you make them pay or don't you?"

"If I made them pay I'd be a whore and your mother's not a whore."

"Then you're just plain dumb."

"I'm a woman, and that's that, and I can't help it if I need a man in my bed. I got married because I thought that was the most practical way. I happened to pick a half-impotent good-for-nothing who spent his time in saloons and came home only to vomit."

"That's no reason."

"No reason for what?"

"Nothing."

It was obvious that he had something on his mind, but he checked his anger and chewed away glumly.

"If you're not satisfied with your mother, go get another one. Aren't you ashamed to talk the way you did in front of your sister?"

He looked at Alice and opened his mouth, but managed to control himself and said nothing. It was only as he left the kitchen that they heard him mutter:

"They're all whores, all of them!"

Twenty years later, Vladimir was to admit to Louis that the night before that Sunday he had had his first disappointment in love, that he had found his girl, the one with whom he went out and on whom he spent his money, in a corner with a man who was making love to her standing up.

He had pulled away the man's overcoat, which was hiding them, and he had seen. He was determined to fight. The other fellow had run away as fast as his legs could carry him, and suddenly Vladimir, who was chasing him, had stopped hearing his footsteps. The man must have been hiding in the shadow of an alley, of which there were many in the neighborhood. Perhaps he had rushed into the first house he came to and was sitting on the stairs waiting.

Vladimir had searched for a long time. The girl had gone home.

"I'd have killed him," he admitted.

He also admitted that for the first time in his life he had cried, he who, as a child, had forbidden himself to shed tears, to let anyone hear him complain.

They got used to the new lighting, which was less intimate than that of the kerosene lamp. Instead of there being a limited circle of light surrounded by a zone of shadow, even the nooks and corners of the two rooms received the same white brightness, which revealed wounds.

They suddenly realized that the walls were dirty, that the mattresses had been patched many times, here and there with cloths of different colors. The ceiling was cracked, and a broad streak of bright white plaster showed where the gas tube went.

Was it that winter? The following winter? Louis could not remember, not knowing whether he had been in the third or fourth grade, for the teacher had changed classes at the same time as the pupils. Louis was always first, though he sat at his desk as dreamily as ever.

He had happened to find, quite by chance, the colored pencils that the Czech had given him for Christmas and that he used to keep in his school bag.

The teacher did not resemble the one he had had in the lower grades. He was thin and had a long, curled mustache and long, narrow goatee which he would tug at nervously. He had very beautiful long, white hands with carefully trimmed nails. He probably earned little money, like the other teachers, but nonetheless made an effort to be elegant. Though his tail coat was rather worn, it was well cut and did not come from a ready-made clothing store. His collars and cuffs were almost always clean and his shoes were of fine leather.

Louis had at first annoyed him with his placidness, with his smile, which the teacher perhaps thought ironic. Then he began to observe him more closely. He would loom up behind Louis when he was writing a composition, would question him point-blank while pretending to look elsewhere.

It was as if Louis were a riddle to him and as if he made it a point of honor to solve that riddle. Perhaps he thought he had found the key to it that morning. It was a market day, and Louis, who was drowsy, was listening to the lesson while drawing one of the pear trees in the yard in black and violet.

He had not noticed that the voice of the teacher, whose name was Huguet, had changed its place, that it no longer came from the dais but from the back of the room. Suddenly a familiar hand seized the unfinished drawing.

The odd thing was that M. Huguet did not say anything to him, did not punish him, but about ten days later, during recess, he went over to Louis.

"What are you planning to do when you grow up, Cuchas?"

"I don't know, sir."

"Isn't there anything that tempts you?"

He searched in his mind, trying hard to be sincere, as he always did.

"No, sir," he finally concluded in disappointment.

"Oh."

That was all. At about the same time, a week or two later, his mother was summoned again by the principal. The twins had not set foot in school for three consecutive days. There was talk of the police, of juvenile court.

In the evening, the redheads let the storm break, without flinching. The following noon, they were home for lunch as usual. They did not return in the afternoon. Twice, despite the bad weather, Gabrielle, wrapping her shawl around her, scoured the neighborhood and questioned the storekeepers.

The gas in the kitchen burned almost all night long. It was Vladimir who, before leaving for work in the morning, thought of the cooky box. There were six of the boxes, with different designs, on a shelf.

The one with a picture of a mill contained the flour, the one with Millet's "Angelus" the sugar, and so on for the coffee and bags of spices, until the last one in the corner, the one painted all over with pompon roses.

That one was the family safe. It contained Gabrielle's marriage booklet, the children's birth certificates, a few yellowing papers that were perhaps old letters, the rent receipts, and now the gas receipts too. In short, that was where their mother kept the family treasures, and also a few dozen francs in a man's billfold and small change for purchases in the neighborhood.

Gabrielle, who had not gone to Les Halles the night before, had already understood.

"Just as I thought. They took the money and left only the bronze coins."

"Vladimir, what should I do?"

She was addressing him as a man for the first time, was asking him for advice as if he had suddenly become the head of the family.

"They won't get very far. Someone'll spot them and inform the police."

"Unless they come back themselves, with the money spent. Where could they have slept in such weather? At least if it were summer!"

"They won't come back by themselves."

"How do you know?"

"I know them better than you. You have to report their disappearance to the police."

"But then they won't give them back to me, especially after what the principal said. They'll be locked up in a reformatory. Vladimir, they're too young!"

Louis was unable to figure out later whether they were eleven or thirteen at the time.

"No hotel will take them without asking them questions. After all, they can't sleep under the bridges."

She was crying, and Alice began crying too. She was the closest to the twins in age, since she was only a year and a half older than they. They had played with her more than with the others and spoke freely in her presence, though they were secretive with the others, because she was a girl.

"It's time for me to go to work. Be sure to go to the police station, Mama. Otherwise you're the one who'll have to explain."

"What do you mean?"

"Nothing. Just go! That's the only way to handle it."

Vladimir had become a man overnight, and their mother felt it so strongly that she started dressing as soon as he left. She had a Sunday dress which she almost never wore and which lasted her three or four years, a lavender-blue silk gown with a yoke and a high lace collar that made her look like a girl, for her face was fresh, without wrinkles, and she was always ready to laugh.

Instead, she put on her everyday clothes and threw her black shawl around her shoulders.

"Don't forget to leave for school on time, Louis. If the principal asks you any questions, say that you don't know where your brothers are."

She was still sniffling as she left the room, but her attitude was bolder, and in the street she held her head high as if she were already confronting the chief. The principal did not send for Louis. Did he even know that young Cuchas and the Heurteau brothers were members of the same family? They were only names among others on his rolls, and he knew only the pupils whom he had to discipline.

It was cold. It was raining. Rubbish was flowing down both sides of the gutter when Louis got home for lunch. Perhaps there was just as much rubbish other days, but on that particular day he noticed it. For him, it was a colorless day, a tasteless day, a day without the usual sounds. He walked in a vacuum, and when he saw his mother and sister sit down at the table in the kitchen, he asked no questions, feeling that they had no good news to report.

"Did anyone say anything to you, Louis?"

"No, Mama."

"I went to the police station."

"I know."

"They're going to try to find them. They were polite. They even offered me a seat. Here's Vladimir! Sit down and start eating.

"I was telling your brother that they were polite and that the chief asked me to sit down. He probably has children, because he understood right away and when I suddenly couldn't keep from crying, he came over and patted me on the shoulder.

"They're going to do what they can. It seems they won't find them in Paris. They're used to that kind of thing. Runaways, as they call them, are reported to them every week.

"They asked me if we'd ever lived in the country, if we went there on vacation or if we had relatives there, because that's where children almost always go when they run away from home. Most of them take the train, often a freight train.

"I asked him if they'd be locked up and he said he didn't think so, that I was known in the neighborhood as an honest tradeswoman who's never violated police regulations."

"You see!"

"I did the right thing in following your advice. There'll always be the chief to defend us."

"Didn't he talk to you about me?"

"Why? Do you know him?"

"Is he a stout man who has a watch chain with charms on it?"

"That's right. You mean you were taken to the police station, and you never told us?"

"I was a kid. I was about Louis's age and a cop caught me swiping a handful of candies from a stand. He picked me up like a rug and took me to the station. The chief put on a gruff voice. I cried and begged him not to tell you because you had enough troubles without that."

"Well I'll be damned!"

She was so dumfounded that she forgot about the twins. It was not until two days later that they were brought back from Rouen, where they had been found huddled behind crates in a freight train. They had thought the train was going to Le Havre, where they were planning to stow away on a boat. They had picked the wrong car, which had been disconnected at Rouen.

They gave no details about their adventure, spent an afternoon in the police station, and the wallet was put back in its place in the box with the pompon roses. Only two francs were missing.

V

"LISTEN TO ME, Guy and Olivier. The rest of you too, because what concerns them concerns all of you."

Gabrielle was weary. Although events usually left few traces on her and she quickly regained her good humor, the twins' escapade had left its mark on her. She was limp. The children could see, if not how discouraged she felt, at least how tired she was.

"I had another talk with the chief today. I beg you, Guy, don't look off into space that way as if it didn't concern you. It's a matter of your future, and your brother's too. He's really taken your situation to heart. The school doesn't want to take you back.

"He thinks there's no point in sending you to another one. You'll soon be thirteen and you'll never get your diploma. I don't have one either, neither does my mother, nor lots of boys who've made good. So, to avoid the reformatory, he advises me to apprentice you. He's found an employer who'll take you, M. Cottin, the printer on Rue Cardinal-Lemoine."

That was beyond Place de la Contrescarpe, Louis's frontier, in a world where he hardly ever ventured.

"I'm warning you that M. Cottin is strict, but I've been told he's fair and that he's decent to his workmen. The chief first thought of separating you. I begged him not to. I assured him you wouldn't be able to bear it. Do you want to become printers?"

They both shrugged.

"I think that's your best bet. Don't you agree, Vladimir?"

"It's sure better than the reformatory."

"Well, you start Monday morning. Tomorrow we'll go and buy the clothes you need."

It seemed to Louis that there was a different atmosphere in the home that evening, a certain constraint, an emotion difficult to define. Was it perhaps the end of a certain kind of existence?

Until then they had lived with each other as in a burrow, sheltered from the outside world, and come what may, their mother was there to protect them. The mattresses, lined up against the wall, formed one big bed, and their mother, though there was usually a man with her, was separated from them only by a bedsheet that hung from a rod.

There was a beginning and an end, the wooden bed on one side and Emilie's little cot on the other, with the whole brood between the two.

The cot had disappeared at the same time as Emilie. Vladimir had become a man. He appeared at meal time only occasionally and led a life of his own about which they knew almost nothing.

Alice, who was fifteen, had already hinted a few times that she was bored being alone in the house for hours on end and that someday she would look for a job. She had become a young lady who went dancing in the evening and brought home foreign odors.

And when the twins started working for M. Cottin, Louis would be the only one who went to school.

Oddly enough, he bore a grudge against the gas. It seemed to him that ever since that hard white light had been installed in the two rooms their life had changed and that part of their intimacy, of the warmth of the burrow, had disappeared. Even the god-stove, on which too much light fell, no longer had its good-natured animal look and one could barely perceive the sparkling of the ashes that fell through the grate from time to time in a fine rain.

Was that the thing that brought him closer to his mother, that impelled him to go to Les Halles with her more often, to spend a few moments near her pushcart when he got out of school? In the years that followed there were bonds between them that had not existed before.

He had become the last of the brood, the last little one. She said so implicitly one day when Vladimir asked why they didn't move to a more comfortable apartment where he could have a room. He felt a need to have a room of his own. He did not even have a closet but shared the hanging wardrobe with his mother, brothers, and sister.

"What's the point?" Gabrielle had replied. "You won't be staying with us much longer and you'll be called up for military service in a few years. Alice, I'm sure of it, will marry at the earliest opportunity. The twins are working and don't come home for lunch."

Louis would often stop in front of the laundry with the pale blue front. Its door was always open, and from it there escaped a special smell, almost as agreeable as that of the bakery. Like most of the shops on the street, this had a narrow front but was very deep, and five or six women worked side by side ironing linen on a long table covered with white thick cotton. Behind them stood a special stove with sloping surfaces on which they heated their irons. Most of them were young, and in summer they probably wore nothing under their white smocks, for he could see their breasts swaying and their hips rolling freely with every movement.

86

He knew that the name of the woman who ran the laundry was Mme. Antoine, that she had started as an apprentice, and that most of the time she stayed in a room at the back where she tagged the linen and made out bills.

The washing was done in the basement, in a cellar crowded with big tanks whose ventilators opened on the yard.

Toward the beginning of autumn, Alice decided to take a job in Mme. Antoine's laundry.

From then on, there was no longer a particular time for meals. Had there ever really been one? They all came home at different times. They knew where the bread was. They found cheese, ham, or liver pâté in the larder, which was a crate that Vladimir had covered with wire screening and fixed outside, on the window sill.

On Sundays, Gabrielle continued to prepare a special dish, boiled beef, lamb stew, or, more rarely, a chicken that she had managed to get cheap. Yet even on Sunday the whole family seldom ate together, especially if the weather was good.

Vladimir dressed like a man and had bought at the Samaritaine Department Store a fashionable black-and-white-checked suit with a short jacket which he wore with a stiff collar and a bow tie.

In summer, he sported a broad-brimmed straw hat, which he wore tilted, and for several months he could be seen twirling a cane.

His area of operation had been spreading for some time, and Rue Mouffetard was now merely a dormitory for him. He would take the train to spend his days off on the banks of the Seine, at Saint-Cloud or Bougival, and spoke of buying a bicycle as soon as he had put enough money aside.

Alice also wore a straw hat, with a much broader brim and adorned with a red ribbon, the ends of which fell down her back.

"Children, where do you expect me to get all that money?"

There had never been so much talk of money before the

older children started working. Alice had bought, for the summer, a white dress trimmed with English embroidery, and, as winter approached, she dreamed of a velvet dress that she had seen in the window of the shop run by the Pochon sisters.

On Saturday night, she would go with girl friends to Bullier's, a big dance hall at the far end of Boulevard Saint-Michel, where she met students. The next day she always had a story to tell. She would be very excited and would mention names that meant nothing to the family: Valérie, Olga, Suzanne, Eugène, Roland.

"Roland is the nicest of the lot. He's at the university, where he's studying to be a lawyer, like his father. His father's the one who defended the anarchists who threw a bomb in front of the Royal Tavern."

There was a great deal of talk about anarchists and bombs, about the subway, a network of tunnels under the streets of Paris where there would be trains that were faster than the omnibuses. Nobody in the family read newspapers. Vladimir would occasionally bring home installments of a kind of magazine entitled *Nick Carter,* the cover of which showed a square-jawed man threatening someone with his revolver or freeing a girl who was tied to a tree or the foot of a bed.

Opposite Saint Médard's Church was a newspaper stand around which other publications hung from clothespins, for example *Le Petit Parisien Illustré,* which described, with violently colored illustrations, the crimes of the week, an old man strangled on Rue Caulaincourt, the woman poisoner of the Ternes neighborhood . . .

All of this began to exist for Louis on the fringes of his life. Before that time, the world was limited to a closed space which had little by little expanded without his realizing it, somewhat as it had for the twins, who now spent almost all their Sundays on the ramparts.

This reminded him of one of his rare conversations with his mother, for when they went to Les Halles together they spoke very little, despite the fact that the market was a long way off. Louis had never wondered what his mother thought about, though he had noticed that she was not engrossed, as he was, in the spectacle of the street.

She would cross the Seine at the Pont Saint-Michel without being aware of the color of the light that day or whether there was a current, and she had probably never really looked at the towers of Notre Dame.

She worked. All grownups worked, except landlords like M. and Mme. Doré or rich people who would go horseback riding, ride in carriages, go to the races in gray top hats, and dine in restaurants with velvet seats and crystal chandeliers.

It was only recently that he had begun to realize this, only since he had started going to the newsstand from time to time to look at the illustrated periodicals.

"What are you thinking about, Louis?"

"Nothing, Mama."

She pushed the cart along a few more yards of pavement, looking straight ahead with her lovely blue eyes.

"You're an odd little fellow."

There was an intimacy between them which was composed of a vague tenderness that never manifested itself in words or effusiveness but only in shy, furtive glances or certain intonations.

It was true that he had no recollection of having been cuddled in her arms, the way children were in the books he read. Perhaps when he was a baby? He retained a vague image of his mother holding Emilie against her bosom, but it was in order to suckle her.

"Are you really thinking about nothing?"

"I don't know."

"It seems one's always thinking about something, even when a person doesn't realize it. I don't remember who told me that, someone who'd been to school."

They walked on a little. A red and yellow streetcar went by

them with a clatter. Louis was fascinated by the streetcars, mainly because of their colors, which enlivened the streets, and also because of the tinkling bells with which they warned pedestrians and the blue sparks they sometimes threw off at the top of their current collectors.

He had recently begun to venture at nightfall as far as Boulevard Saint-Michel just to watch them go by, for it was nicer in the darkness. All he could see of the people who rode in them was their top hats and heads, as in a Punch and Judy show. They sat silently in a row, side by side, with fixed stares, in the diffuse light of another world, and at every jolt the heads would all bend to the same side before slowly straightening up.

"When your brothers and sister were your age, and even long before, they never stopped asking questions. Don't you ask questions in school either?"

He had to think. The world of school was so far away from that of the market.

"No, Mama."

"What about your friends?"

"I don't have any friends."

"Don't you ever play with the other pupils?"

"No."

"Is it that they don't want to play with you?"

He was embarrassed by her trying, for no apparent reason, to penetrate his secret world. It wasn't a world, but rather a picture book, perhaps a silly one, but he didn't feel like talking about it.

"Don't you like to play?"

"I do play."

"All by yourself?"

"Sometimes I play chess."

"That's no game for a young boy."

"I've played marbles, I've played with my top, I've rolled a hoop."

Not for very long, but he had played.

"You never laugh. Are you happy, Louis?"

"Very happy, Mama."

"Wouldn't you rather have been born in another family? Isn't there anything you miss?"

"I've got you."

She looked at him in amazement, her eyes shining.

"You really love me?"

"I do, Mama."

If she had not had to push her cart and if they had not already entered Rue des Halles, where it was impossible to stop in the midst of the traffic, she would probably have kissed him or hugged him to her beautiful bosom. She forced a laugh, a muffled laugh.

"You don't really mean that I'm enough for you?"

"You are, Mama."

"You're the most charming boy in the world. If only you continue to be happy. If only I could guess what goes on in your mind! With Vladimir, with your sister, even with Guy and Olivier, however tight-lipped they are, I think I can figure them out and I'm seldom wrong. But you, you're a mystery. And yet —I oughtn't to say so—you're the one I like best . . ."

She could not prevent herself from adding:

"Although Vladimir . . ."

As if Vladimir, for her, were in a class apart. He was born when she was very young, and she was pregnant with him when she married Heurteau. Vladimir belonged to another race, so much so that though the name on his birth certificate was Joseph, he was always called Vladimir. Was Vladimir the name of his real father? Was he a Russian? Had she loved him? Had he abandoned her?

Questions floated across his mind, as they also did in later years, but he did not really put them to himself. He considered them unimportant and never did anything to find an answer to them.

They had entered Samuel's huge shed, and his mother, who

was looking up at the blackboard, seemed ashamed of their un-usual conversation.

"What should I get today?"

The blackboard had become familiar to Louis. As soon as they entered the area of the market, his watchful eyes observed the piles of fruit and vegetables, his mind noted the prices written on the labels and those that were yelled out by the fiercely competitive vendors.

"Apples, Mama."

"Why apples?"

"Because they're red, the kind that children like best. They're not expensive today."

He did not add that he admired the crimson color of the pippins, the golden, star-shaped designs that illuminated their skin, their slightly flattened shape.

"How much can I have the apples for, Samuel?"

"How many crates?"

"Enough to make a big pile on the cart. On Rue Mouffetard, the more there are, the more they attract people. They think you're selling them cheap because you're afraid to have any left over."

It was true. He had seen his mother waiting for hours trying to sell a few bunches of leeks that were left at the bottom of the pushcart, whereas when it was overflowing with them she didn't know where to turn first.

"If you knock off two sous, I'll take ten crates."

He felt she wanted to please him and it bothered him all morning in school. At noon, he ran to find out how the apples were selling and was overjoyed to see from a distance that the pyramid had melted. His mother was very vivacious.

"You see, my boy, you've brought me luck. Here! Go buy yourself a bar of chocolate."

She gave him a sou, which he dared not refuse, but he was sorry to be rewarded, particularly since he didn't deserve to be, because it wasn't she he had thought of but the apples. He nevertheless bought the chocolate and licked it as he walked up the street. His sister's voice yelled out to him as he passed the laundry.

"Did Mama give you some money? Why?"

"Because I advised her to buy apples and she's sold almost all of them."

It must have been autumn. The weather was almost as warm as in summer and there were broad rings of sweat under Alice's arms. Only the two of them would be home for lunch. When things were selling well, their mother preferred to get rid of the whole stock before going home and contented herself with a snack, a chunk of bread and a few slices of salami, plus two or three visits to the saloon opposite to gulp down a glass of wine.

"Which would you rather have, Louis? Dutch cheese or camembert?"

"Isn't there anything else?"

"There's some currant jam left, but you know Mama doesn't like us to eat it at noon."

"Then camembert."

It was a coincidence. It was not a legend that he created later as others were to create legends about his childhood. The chocolate was a point of reference. Louis was not particularly fond of chocolate. It was Vladimir who, when he was Louis's age, had eaten it whenever he could treat himself. When his mother handed Louis the coin, she must have confused him with his brother. When he sat down to eat, he still had the taste of the chocolate in his mouth, so that the camembert seemed less good to him than usual.

His mother had almost indulged in confidences that morning, had displayed more tenderness to him than usual, and he had the impression that she loved him as if he were a warm, soft kitten that was still defenseless.

As they sat and ate face to face, his sister looked sometimes at the window and sometimes at her brother, with a hesitant air.

"Listen, Louis. I think you like me and that I've never done you any harm."

She was nibbling without appetite and spoke in a forced manner.

"You're a nice boy, you can keep a secret. I've got to tell it to someone and I don't dare say a word to Vladimir or Mama. Vladimir would blow up. And as for Mama . . ."

He waited. He felt embarrassed by the role of confidant, just as he had felt that morning.

"Louis, I think I'm pregnant."

She was surprised at his being unperturbed, as if there were nothing startling or dramatic about the news.

"Do you hear? Don't you realize what that means?"

"Of course I realize. You're going to have a child."

"I wonder whether I ought to let it happen. I'm not quite sixteen."

"Mama wasn't much older when she had Vladimir."

"It's not the same."

"Why?"

"I wouldn't even be able to tell who the father is. Sylvie, my girl friend at the laundry, has been pregnant twice. She went both times to see a midwife in the neighborhood who got rid of it for her. She didn't suffer at all the first time and didn't miss a day's work. But the second time, she was so sick that she had to see a doctor who had to do a curettage. All the same, she advises me to go to the midwife. I'm scared, Louis! What would you do if you were in my boots?"

"Nothing."

"You'd let it happen?"

"Of course."

"Even if it meant messing up my life?"

He felt she was annoyed with him for his seeming indifference. What else could he have said to her? Alice would have a child, and that was that.

Time passed quickly during that period. He had known long periods, of endless weeks, winters that went on and on though people talked about spring and buds every day. He had known short spells that brought you back to school, which seemed only to have just ended.

This one was a very brief period, and the seasons were so mixed up that later he was unable to determine when things had happened.

He was to remember evenings he had spent waiting for his sister to talk to their mother finally about the child, for ever since she had let him in on the secret he could see that she was getting bigger, that her face was pale, that she had a resigned look.

At the same time he noticed that his mother was receiving fewer and fewer men. Perhaps she even no longer had regular lovers who lounged in bed in the morning, ate with them, and came back in the evening as if they were members of the family.

The twins would come home from work tired, with their fingernails black and their clothes smelling of lead and printer's ink, and would go to bed early. They went to the shop regularly. M. Cottin would not have tolerated absence. Their attitude nevertheless remained grim and they had a shifty look. They did what they had to do, because there was no getting around it, but they felt like prisoners and someday they would take their revenge.

"Aren't you sleepy, Louis?"

There were only three of them in the kitchen, his mother, his sister, and he. As he did not answer at once, Alice signaled to him and he understood. She was going to talk.

She closed the door behind him. He felt uneasy and did not fall asleep immediately. He expected to hear shouting.

The conversation began in a monotone. There were only some indistinct sounds, and he woke up in the morning without knowing anything of what had followed. He had not heard his mother get up, but she was no longer in bed. His three brothers, who started work at seven o'clock, had left. Alice began at half past six. So he was alone in the house, as often happened when he did not accompany his mother to Les Halles.

There was some coffee left in the flowered coffeepot beside the fire. He ate quickly so as to have time to run down the block before going to school. He saw Alice ironing with the other girls. She was the third in line, and since he pressed his face against the window she finally caught sight of him. She smiled and nodded in a way that meant it's all right, that is, that the thing had gone off smoothly.

Almost immediately, or so it seemed to him, her pregnancy became obvious, and he wondered whether she wasn't exaggerating it deliberately by tightening her dresses at the waist. She walked with her head tilted slightly back, as if to resist the weight of her belly, which nevertheless was still quite small.

"Have you heard the news, Louis?" asked his mother when he went to see her at the pushcart after school.

"I have, Mama."

"Are you glad you're going to be an uncle?"

"I am, Mama."

Vladimir, knitting his thick black eyebrows, was the only one who displayed resentment toward his sister.

"You're dumb enough to have done it on purpose! You think you're playing with a doll."

For Alice had bought wool, knitting needles, and a magazine with colored illustrations entitled *Layettes* and had begun to knit in the evening, which did not prevent her from going dancing at Bullier's the next Saturday and the following Saturdays.

As for their mother, though she no longer received men, she began to go out at night, on Saturday too, so that Louis stayed

96

home alone that day. She dressed up in a way that, in the past, she had done only on rare occasions. She would take her lavender-blue silk dress out of its cardboard box and iron it, and also her petticoats, and she wore a corset that Louis had to help her lace.

"I'm getting fat," she remarked. "If I continue, I'll be enormous. You'd think it was due to my work."

She had partly unstitched the famous dress in order to let it out, and even then it was tight on her. After powdering her face, putting on make-up, and sprinkling herself with carnation perfume, she would kiss Louis on the forehead.

"Good night, my little man. You're nice, you know! I hope you won't think too badly of me when you're older."

A few weeks later, Alice had time to explain to him, while knitting slippers that resembled doll's slippers:

"Mama was swell. I offered, for her sake and the whole family's, to go to the country and work on a farm or at an inn where they'd have surely taken me on for my board. You could have simply told people that I was tired and you had sent me to live with relatives out of town, or to a sanitarium. I'd have given birth and left the child at a baby farm and no one would have known anything. Mama said no right away, that I had nothing to be ashamed of, that all the storekeepers on the street, including the most stuck-up, had their first child before they were married or only four or five months later.

"She said to me, 'Daughter, look them straight in the face. Carry your egg in front of you like a real female and be sure not to lower your eyes.' "

Public works were going on all over Paris and streets were being torn up. Electricity was being installed everywhere. One Saturday evening when his mother had not got dressed up, Louis asked her: "May I go to the Belle Jardinière Department Store?"

"It's closed by now."

"I know, but I'd like to see the arc lamps."

97

They talked about the lights in school. They talked about lots of things that he didn't know, about the Eiffel Tower, for example, which he had seen only from a distance, though most of his classmates had been to the top of it.

In summer, many of them took the train to spend their vacation at the home of grandparents or aunts who lived in the country. At least two boys in his class had relatives in Caen and had seen the ocean.

He himself had not been on a streetcar. He was not bitter about it, was in no hurry to have new experiences, did not try to widen his universe. Perhaps everything outside of that limited circle even frightened him. He let the world come to him, little by little, bit by bit.

"Would you like me to go with you?"

"I'd be pleased, but if you've got something to do I know the way."

Whenever he went to Les Halles, he saw the department stores and, from a distance, the wax dummies frozen in strange postures.

It was an unforgettable evening.

"You want me to dress up?"

He dared not answer either yes or no. She dressed as carefully as she did when she went out on a date, sprayed herself with the same carnation perfume, dabbed her face with the pink powder, and put on lipstick.

"Don't I look too old?"

"Oh no!" he exclaimed fervently.

She locked the door and put the key under the mat. In the street she suddenly said to him:

"Take my arm, as if you were my sweetheart."

That had never happened to them. He made himself walk on tiptoe, for he had not grown much. If they had met Vladimir, he would have snickered, whereas the redheads would have looked away.

"Shall we take the streetcar to the Châtelet?"

All the lights were dancing in his head. For the first time, he saw people sitting at lighted sidewalk cafés in the evening. In the streetcar, he held his breath so as not to lose the tiniest bit of his emotion, and he smiled vaguely at the lady in black who looked funny when the movement of the car jolted her from side to side. At times she looked as if she were about to doze off and suddenly, just as her head grazed her neighbor's shoulder, she would open her eyes in astonishment.

He saw the famous arc lamps, big globes that shed a bright, bluish light that quivered and crackled. When you stared at one and then closed your eyes, you saw ten, twenty globes in your head and it took a long time for them to go out.

"In the spring, if all goes well, I'll buy you a suit like that one."

A wax boy with painted hair was wearing a sailor suit with a big white-trimmed collar. He looked as if he were taking a step forward, with his hand out to receive something, and was wearing patent-leather shoes.

"Come. I'll treat you to a drink."

His mother would occasionally buy him a glass of soda in the saloons around Les Halles where she would have a glass of wine to give her a lift, but he had never set foot in a real café. There was one opposite the Châtelet with mirrors on the walls and tables with white marble tops. He looked at the crowd anxiously, wondering whether there would be room.

Lots of men stared at his mother as she went by and some of them threw her seductive smiles. She was resplendent. She seemed beautiful to him in the light of the chandeliers that livened her face and made her eyes sparkle and the silk of her dress shine.

"A grenadine syrup for my son and an apricot cordial for me."

The words were also new to him. He realized that his mother, whom he usually saw pushing her cart, frequented such places. She was completely at ease.

Although she had almost reproached him for not asking questions, he did ask one. There was an object that fascinated him much more than the mirrors and the ceiling on which naked women were painted, much more than the long white and gold bar where the waiters went to pick up the drinks and where a cashier with a cameo on her black dress sat like a queen. The object was a big, bright metal globe at the end of a metal stem.

There was not only one but four of them, in different parts of the vast café.

"Say, Mama, what are those globes for?"

Perhaps he was disappointed by her reply:

"For the dishcloths."

He got his diploma. Instead of being first, as he had been the other years, he was only third. He had worked neither more nor less than usual. Perhaps he had been more fascinated by the outer world.

His sister, whose belly had grown bigger and whose features had become somewhat puffy, had stopped working on the layette.

"Actually it's cheaper to buy it in a store."

The truth was that she had acquired a taste for reading. She had discovered a bookstore on Boulevard du Port-Royal which had stalls on the sidewalk, the kind one saw on the quays.

The cheap novels that she read had colored covers, like the illustrated Sunday papers. They cost sixty-five centimes, and after reading them one could exchange them for others by paying an additional ten centimes. Most of them were dirty, dog-eared, and spotted with grease, but their coarse, yellowish paper had a good smell. She sometimes read as many as three a week, especially toward the end, when she could no longer stand on her feet and iron all day.

Occasionally, when her legs were very tired, she would ask Louis to go and exchange a book for her.

"What kind do you want?"

"You know, a sad one."

She was not sad herself and was delighted at the idea of having her baby.

"I think Mama's right. If I keep it here, I won't be able to work any more or go out in the evening. I'm too young to live in two rooms with a baby and it's better for both the child and me to send it to a farm. To say nothing of the fact that the open air will be good for it and that I'll go to see it every Sunday."

There were some feverish days. They would buy the newspaper in order to see the classified ads and would discuss them in the evening.

"Meaux! It's nice, but it's too far from Paris. Imagine how far I'd have to go just to take the train."

They considered Sartrouville, Corbeil, and a village near Etampes, and finally chose a place run by a Mme. Campois in Meudon. It was only a few minutes by train from Montparnasse Station. Vladimir had a regular girl friend and did not go with them. Neither did the twins, who had organized a gang on the ramparts and attacked a rival gang every Sunday.

Their mother had put on her pretty dress. Alice, who was in blue, was wearing a broad straw hat with a ribbon attached under the chin to prevent it from being blown away by the wind. Louis rode in a streetcar for the second time, went through the gate of the station, and climbed into a third-class carriage filled with soldiers in red trousers.

In Clamart they had difficulty finding the way that Mme. Campois had indicated in her letter, or rather in the letter she had had a neighbor write for her.

They first went in the wrong direction. The road was covered with a thick layer of dust into which their feet sank. The cornfields were dotted with poppies. The weather was warm. Their skin smelled good. Everything smelled good, the air, the meadows, the barns that they passed, the cows.

They stopped at a farm to ask directions and continued on

their way, feeling weak in the knees and overcome by the sun. Finally they saw a man in leather boots and a brown corduroy outfit who was standing at the side of the road and seemed to be waiting.

"Mme. Heurteau? Did you have much trouble finding us? It's because we're in an out-of-the-way spot here."

He pointed down to a house with a pink roof and white-washed walls. The apple trees were laden with fruit. The grass was bright. Two goats came over to look at them before capering off, as if inviting them to play.

"Are they yours?" asked Alice excitedly.

"Yes, they are. We've got a few animals. After all, my wife has to keep busy."

Chickens were foraging around the white house. There were also ducks and two big ungainly geese, and a few yards from the house was a pond covered with duckweed.

"Rosalie!" called the man.

She emerged from a low room, whitewashed like the rest of the house, and put on her nicest smile. She had a beaming face, enormous breasts, and hips that rolled when she started walking. In the kitchen was a youngster about a year and a half old who was sitting on the floor.

"He's my first. I nursed him at the same time as Dr. Dubois's grandson. My husband's the doctor's coachman. I had so much milk that I could have fed three. Come inside. Sit down and have something."

The chairs were straw-bottomed. They did not see a stove, but there were ashes in the fireplace where an iron hook was hanging.

"When are you due?" asked Rosalie, looking at Alice's belly like a connoisseur.

"Probably in two weeks."

"Well, if you ask me, it could happen tonight or tomorrow, or the day after tomorrow at the latest. Don't you think so, Léonard? Come take a look in here."

Opening a door, she showed them a huge room with windows on both sides, a bed with a white coverlet, and two wicker cradles adorned with tulle flounces that seemed to be waiting. In the opposite corner, next to an enormous wardrobe, was the child's little bed.

"That way, you realize, I can always keep an eye on them. If we agree about terms, you can bring it to me whenever you like, and Dr. Dubois can tell you he'll be taken good care of."

Léonard allowed Louis to pick apples from one of the trees in the orchard and pulled down a branch so that he could reach it.

"Take a lot of them. As many as you want. There's quite a crop this year. Would you like to see the rabbits?"

There was a hutch full of them and others too in a square of grass surrounded by wire netting where they sat motionless, except for the mechanical movement of their cheeks.

"Would you like to live in the country?"

"I don't know."

"Do you prefer Paris?"

"I don't know."

His mother was served a small glass of brandy. Alice dipped a lump of sugar into it. Louis was given a glass of cold water that was drawn from the well in a wooden bucket.

His mother woke him when the train reached Montparnasse Station. His cheeks were burning and his eyes were feverish. It seemed to him that an important event had just occurred, that the protective cocoon in which he had been enveloped had suddenly cracked, and he felt both heavy-laden and lighthearted.

Part Two

The Little Boy of
Rue de l'Abbé-de-l'Epée

I

DATES HARDLY MATTERED in the family. There was no calendar on the wall. They reckoned rather by season, Gabrielle by the fruits and vegetables that succeeded each other on the push-cart, cherries, strawberries, string beans, and the first peas, peaches which were less expensive in midsummer, apples in the autumn, cabbages and oyster plants in winter.

The appearance or disappearance of charcoal burners on the sidewalk was also a sign, as were the days when there was no market because excessive cold, or fog, which remained a subject of conversation for a long time, or ice on the streets or a heavy snow would have made it impossible for the peddlers to get their loaded carts back from the market and because, in addition, housewives did not go out in such weather.

Gabrielle could not have told the children's dates of birth without consulting the official papers that were yellowing in the cooky box, and in order to measure time they would refer to memorable events: the year when the Seine had frozen, the year of Emilie's death, the autumn when gas had been installed, the period in which Vladimir had started working as an apprentice for M. Brillanceau.

Others were added as the children grew up. Some points of reference were common to all of them, others had special meaning for individual members of the family.

In the case of Louis, for example, it was not so much the birth of Alice's child that mattered as his first train trip. The things that constituted his discovery of life, Vladimir looking through the hole in the sheet, then his sister's blonde hair on her naked belly, were more important than Alice's marriage to a boy named Gaston Cottereau who worked in a delicatessen on Rue de Rennes.

There was also the gap between the little ones and the big ones and the one between the children and the mother, which had varied several times. For example, Vladimir had been a little one at a time when a certain man was living regularly in the apartment, and he must have remembered it, whereas for Louis Vladimir had always been a big boy. He himself remembered only men who came and went, smells, voices, the different footsteps of those who stayed three days and those who stayed a month, of those who ate with them and those he saw only in the evening, so that Pliska, who was only a vague figure in the memory of Vladimir and Alice, remained an important personage for him.

Louis was perhaps the only one, in addition to his mother, for whom little Emilie, of whom they never spoke, had had a real existence, because at that time he spent the whole day at home.

Vladimir and Alice were the eldest. They understood each other and exchanged secrets. Then Vladimir had suddenly become a man whom his mother asked for advice, whereas Alice remained a girl for a while and the difference in age between her and the twins and then between her and Louis mattered less and less.

It wasn't his first day in school that counted but the first time he had been beaten up there, when he had refused to give up his marbles. His school record no longer existed, though he could still see the hand of the teacher, whose name he had difficulty in remembering, suddenly coming down over his shoulder and seizing the drawing he had just made of one of the chestnut trees in the yard.

Was it M. Charles? No. M. Charles was the big fellow with the flabby mouth. It was M. Huguet.

The twins' escapade, the first one, the one that had ended in Rouen, had no date, could not be placed. The discovery of Les Halles as he clung to his mother's apron strings was more precise in time and space.

Then there was the conversation with his mother on a bench in a little park where pigeons came begging for bread, which they had not thought of bringing.

Why had they been in a park around the middle of the afternoon? He would have been unable to tell, just as he could not remember the name of the park, which was not far from a hospital.

Yet he had not been a small child at the time. He recalled details of the period when he was six or seven, but certain details of this experience remained hazy.

"You're intelligent, Louis. You learn things easily. You're the only one of us who has a diploma. Tell me frankly, would you like to go on with your studies?"

"I don't think so, Mama."

"Have you thought of what you want to do later on?"

"Not exactly."

"What about now? You're less strong than your brothers. I can't see you working in a shop or on a scaffold. If you feel like continuing, don't worry about money. Your brothers are starting to earn wages. I've got good customers and I'm strong on my feet."

"Thanks, Mama, but I don't feel like it."

"You can't go on indefinitely following me to the market in the morning and daydreaming the rest of the day."

"I'd like to work at the market. For M. Samuel."

"What would you do there?"

"Last year I saw a kid who carried slips of paper from one end of the shed to the other and did errands outside."

"The Flea!"

"I could do the same thing."

M. Samuel never wore a jacket or a collar. He was stout and short-legged and his big belly overflowed his trousers, which were held up by pale blue suspenders. The number of folds of his chin varied, depending on whether he was looking up or down, and a tiny black cap sat perched on the top of his bald pate. With a pencil in his ear, he sat in state in the middle of his shed, the importance of which was not suspected by the people who walked up Rue Coquillière during the day. To them it was only a porte-cochère.

At night, one noticed the glass vault, as in railway stations, piled-up cases, crates and bags. Three clerks, one of whom was a woman, worked without stop in the glass cage. Pushcarts entered, threaded their way through the stock, and came out full, while figures were written on the blackboard.

For years, that warehouse, that little stock exchange for small storekeepers and peddlers which was on the margin of the big exchange, the central market of Paris, was going to be Louis's vital element, as water is the element of fish.

He no longer left with his mother between three and six in the morning, depending on the season. He started work at ten in the evening, when men in rags began wandering around looking for a job.

At that hour, the shed was almost empty. There was only the food that had been unsold the day before. Samuel, with his pencil in his ear, would wait for the first wagons, which were drawn by broken-down horses, to come in from the Argenteuil flatlands or some other rural area.

At first, the shed was lit by gas, but before long Samuel installed arc lamps which were as bright as the ones Louis had seen at the Belle Jardinière.

"No, Victor. I can't pay that price. You know my customers. They're not people that the sky's the limit for, who slip a rebate to the cook or headwaiter."

He was a weepy type and always tried to play on his clients' feelings.

"I feed simple, ordinary people, people who work hard and who don't know that they owe it to Samuel that they've got peaches on the table, just like the bourgeois, instead of having to settle for hog plums. You fellows from the country imagine there are only rich people in Paris."

He had several refrains in his repertory which he recited without giving anyone time to interrupt.

"Hello, little one. Come take a look here."

For him, Louis was always "the little one," with no other name.

"This little one, for example! I took him on out of charity, because his mother has God knows how many children and she'll be here tonight with her pushcart along with the others. The grandmother's been pushing hers for thirty years. Little one, go ask in the office if Vacher called up about the leeks."

It was true that Samuel did not sell to the stores in the smart neighborhoods but to the vegetable dealers who had only a hole in the wall and a few baskets on the sidewalk and who stayed open until ten at night.

Louis would come back with a slip of paper. Everything was settled by means of slips that were torn from pads in which a sheet of carbon paper made a copy.

"That's another one who takes me for a philanthropist!"

He would pull his pencil from his ear, cross out a figure, and jot down another.

"Tell them they can take it or leave it!"

Louis would go off again to the paved shed where, when no

people were around, his footsteps resounded as in a church. The warehousemen were beginning to receive merchandise. The telephone on the wall, in the glass cage, rang constantly and the clerk would yell into it so as to make himself heard.

"Run over to that bandit Chailloux and tell him . . ."

Rue Rambuteau, Rue de la Ferronnerie, Rue Sainte-Opportune, or one of those huge, spectral sheds. He would worm his way with a bill in his hand and find an agent or wholesaler as busy as Samuel.

They would spend two or three hours that way, buying from each other and keeping posted on the prices, which varied according to what came in, and shortly thereafter the little train from Arpajon would arrive and stop in the street with its freight cars that smelled of the country.

The shed would fill up with merchandise. They would take on a few down-and-outers to carry loads on their back.

The second year, Louis was already given the job of standing near the main door and checking what came in: so many cases of this, so many crates of that. And, of course, jotting down the names of the producers.

Some of the helpers who were taken on for two or three hours and then went to eat a bag of fried potatoes and a dried sausage at the corner of Rue Montmartre were young men who had only recently arrived from a cozy house in the provinces and come up against a Paris that was hard and indifferent.

The others, the old ones, whom one saw staggering out of the saloons after work, had no more illusions.

Women with big behinds walked back and forth on high heels, and they would stop under the lighted globe at the door of a hotel.

At a given moment, the tide rose again. The figures that M. Page chalked on the blackboard changed each time that Louis, who went back and forth between him and the glass cage, brought a new slip of paper. No sooner did the merchandise come in than it started going out, not by the cartload but a few cases at a time. He would recognize his mother among the purchasers and would find time to whisper to her as he rushed by:

"Wait awhile and take carrots."

At 8 A.M. the noise and bustle was over, and a man in a blue apron would wash the tiled floor of the shed with a hose.

"See you tonight, little one."

Louis would go to a bar for a cup of coffee and croissants and would sometimes treat himself to a bag or two of fried potatoes.

When he got home the apartment would be empty, and as soon as he undressed he would flop down on his mattress. The other mattresses had disappeared one by one as discreetly as Emilie's cot.

The first to go was that of Vladimir, who had left for Toulon to do his military service and never understood why he had been assigned to the Marine Corps, since he had never seen the ocean except in photographs. He came home several times on leave, and his wide trousers, blue collar, and tufted cap were quite becoming to him.

He had to pass through Paris several times during his training period, but he did not always visit the apartment on Rue Mouffetard.

One spring, around the month of April, two more mattresses disappeared. The twins, who were about fifteen but as big and strong as boys of twenty, ran away from home for good. They left a note on the kitchen table:

"Don't bother informing the police. We won't be back. Goodby to all of you."

They had both signed it. There were four spelling mistakes in the note. This time they did not take the money from the box but only their birth certificates and whatever linen and clothes they had, which did not make up a bundle too heavy for their shoulders.

The room suddenly looked empty. The curtain was no longer in its place. One day when Gabrielle had been in bed with the grippe, she remarked:

"I wonder why we keep that old bedsheet. It no longer serves any purpose. Louis, don't you think we ought to take it down?"

It was now he whom she asked for advice. He had taken it down, including, though not without difficulty, the rod, which was too firmly fixed.

"Good God, the room looks so big! I didn't remember it as big as this."

No doubt she was imagining it as it had been in the days of her marriage with Heurteau, when there was only Vladimir, who slept on the cot.

In the evening, Alice stopped at the threshold, dumfounded, and likewise exclaimed:

"It's so big!"

No sooner had she lain down than she murmured:

"Say, Mama, would you mind if I slept with you?"

"Aren't you afraid of catching my grippe?"

"You forget that I had it first."

The mattress remained unused for a few days, and one morning, when he got home from work, Louis took it and laid it on the garbage cans in the yard, where the carpenter had been replaced by another one, for the former had committed suicide. He had been found hanging in the cellar after a two-day search, for he had never used it and, as it was summer, no one had gone down to it to get coal. There was a rumor that he had been neurasthenic. Another resident of the street, Ramon, the Spaniards' son, also disappeared. It was Alice who kept her brother informed of what went on, for he hardly spoke to anyone.

"Did you know he was almost thrown in jail?"

Louis showed no surprise.

"Such a good-looking, elegant young man, always so well

groomed. Well, he belonged to a small gang that snatched hand-bags from women who were alone. Two others were also arrested, but we don't know their names because it seems they come from good families. Their parents greased someone's palm and the thing's been hushed up. Ramon's been sent to an uncle in Spain, and his parents tell people that he wanted to enter an officers' training school."

Everything was changing, quickly or gradually, depending on the particular period. Automobiles, which had been such a rarity that people had gone out of their way to see one, became more numerous than horse-drawn carriages and there were as many taximeter cabs in the streets as coaches. People no longer called the subway the Métropolitain, but the Métro, and at times one would see an airplane passing in the sky.

One of the women in high-heeled shoes who walked up and down the sidewalks of Les Halles was younger, smaller, and thinner than the others. She had dark hair and black eyes.

One winter morning, when he had finished working, she had called out to Louis:

"Have you ever tried it, kid?"

He had answered frankly that he hadn't. How had she guessed that he had been wanting to for some time?

"You want me to break you in?"

The expression had shocked him.

"I know how it's done."

"But you still don't know how nice it is. Come along! I feel like doing it with you. You'll give me whatever you like."

She had a room on the fourth floor of the hotel whose globe was always lit at night. It was about fifty yards from the shed.

"You're lucky! Since you're the last and I'm going to bed, you'll see me undressed."

He watched her get ready but kept his clothes on. When she was naked, she lay down on the bed, the coverlet of which was partly protected by oilcloth.

"What are you waiting for? Come here. I'll help you. I bet you're ashamed to show me your tool."

He shook his head hesitantly. He was keenly disappointed but would have liked not to make her feel bad, not to hurt her. A few moments before, when she was undressing, he had desired her. She had made a mistake in taking all her clothes off, in spreading her legs, in exhibiting a slot invaded by long black hairs.

His mother's was delicate, surrounded by a reddish moss which stood out elegantly against the whiteness of her belly.

The other slot which he had often seen, and still saw occasionally, his sister's, was barely shaded with blonde down.

"What's happening to you?"

"I don't know."

"Do I disgust you?"

"No."

"Well, are you or aren't you?"

He shook his head as he stepped back toward the door and stammered:

"I apologize."

"That's the limit. I make you a present because you've been eying me for months when I pass Samuel's place. And the one time I get undressed—which would give the other girls a laugh —I did it because you're a virgin and I thought it would help you. So the gentleman turns up his nose. Tell me, you little snotnose, you half-pint, do you think you're . . ."

He didn't hear the rest of it. He tore down the stairs, frightened at the thought that she might run after him just as she was and keep screaming insults at him and that the doors of the other rooms might open one after the other.

When he got to the street, he walked away fast, and it was not until he reached the Châtelet, where he felt safe, that he remembered he had not eaten.

Standing at the bar of a café whose walls were covered with tiles, he dismally dipped his croissant into his coffee and, for the

116

first time in his life, wondered whether he was like anyone else.

Would he have been able to go through with it if she hadn't had such dark hair and a bushy triangle that went up to her belly button? She had pretty eyes. She had been nice, at first.

She had called him "half-pint." He had been called that by schoolmates and was used to it. But hadn't she given the expression a special meaning?

Perhaps he ought to have tried it the same day with a blonde or a redhead, to set his mind at ease. He remembered what a woman storekeeper on their street had once said to his mother when he still wore his hair long:

"Is it a little boy or a little girl?"

It would be a long time before he tried again. He was afraid of discovering that he was impotent.

He saw no connection between that experience and the event, a much more important one, which took place a few weeks later. Yet the woman's image often came back to him. He dreamed about her several times in the room where he had had to put up a shade, since he slept there during the day.

He even recalled details which he did not remember having noticed, such as the brownness of her nipples and the wide pink band around them. Not only did she have hair high on her belly, but also very low down, on her thighs.

He had twenty-two francs in his pocket that afternoon. Later, in the case of other sums, he was often all at sea, for the value of money changed many times in the course of his life. He earned forty francs a month at Samuel's, which he would turn over to his mother, including the tips from the market gardeners, and Gabrielle would then give him pocket money for the week.

Twenty-two francs represented two months' savings. He had noted the store at the lower end of Rue de Richelieu, not far from the National Library. It was a big stationery firm with two show windows, a whole section of which was reserved for artists' materials and which employed ten clerks in the store alone.

He had often stopped in front of the display, looking at what he called the "colors," for he had no idea of the various mediums, and everything fascinated him, the paints in the little white earthenware bowls lined up in iron boxes, the chalks of softer and gentler tones, the tubes in small chests, which had a palette that fitted into the cover.

It must have been five in the afternoon. He had two ways of spending his days, depending on the weather, how tired he was, his mood of the moment. There were times when he would return to the apartment at about nine in the morning, go straight to bed, and sleep until four or five in the afternoon, as he had done that day.

On other days, he preferred to roam about, sit on a bench, go walking in a new neighborhood, then kiss his mother at the curb, go home to eat, and sleep until evening.

The salesmen and saleswomen wore the same gray smocks. There were three saleswomen, and he waited outside until they were busy with customers before entering the store. Then he went straight to the artists' counter.

"What would you like, young man?"

Because of his height everyone thought he was younger than he was, and people adopted a protective, almost gentle manner with him.

"I'd like some colors, sir."

"Colored pencils?"

"No. I've got some."

He jealously preserved, without quite knowing why, the set that Pliska had once given him. He used them only on rare occasions.

"Watercolors, gouache?"

He hardly dared express his desire, fearing lest the salesman laugh at him.

"The brightest colors."

And, after a hesitation and a furtive glance at the marvels on the shelves, he added:

"Pure colors."

He had uttered the word "pure" in such a tone, with such fervor, that the salesman, a middle-aged man, took an interest in him.

"If I gather correctly, you've never painted?"

"I've drawn at times with colored pencils."

"Has someone seen your drawings and advised you to paint?"

"No one."

"Have you seen many paintings?"

"Never."

He had occasionally stopped in front of picture galleries around Rue de Seine. The paintings on display in the windows had not interested him. It had not occurred to him that one could enter, see the other paintings inside, and leave without buying anything.

"Lots of young people start with water colors."

He showed him an open box of them and picked up another.

"These are in tubes and those in bowls."

"Do the colors stay just as bright?"

"Not quite. Gouache fades less."

"Is it better?"

"It depends on what you want to do. Landscapes? Portraits?"

He dared not say "Everything together," spots, streaks, colors next to each other, the way he saw them in the street, the kind his memory was full of.

"Of course, if you want real brilliance, the only thing is oil paint."

He opened a chest of oils in which at least thirty tubes were set between two metal flasks.

"I don't like some of the colors."

He pointed to them: that one . . . that one . . . that one
. . .

"Why don't you like them?" insisted the salesman, who was amused.

"They're dark and sad. They don't sparkle."

"The simplest thing is to do what painters do. Buy an empty box and a palette, and choose your colors. Come over here and have a look."

He took him to a glass-topped counter that Louis had not noticed, and it seemed to the boy that all the colors in the world were offering themselves to him under the glass.

"May I touch the tubes?"

"Of course."

The salesman pulled back the pane and Louis took out a long, thin tube and read: Veronese green.

"Is that the greenest?"

"There are more than twenty kinds of green. Their brightness depends on the colors around them."

"I understand."

It was true. He had understood, and he spent a quarter of an hour examining the colored circles that indicated the color contained in each tube.

"Is it just the same inside?"

"Exactly the same. Of course, you can mix them on the palette."

The names enchanted him. They were more evocative than the poems he had been taught in school: Naples yellow, burnt sienna, carmine lake, ultramarine . . .

He laid aside those that seemed to him essential, but he would have loved to buy everything in the trays.

"Do you think I have what I need?"

"In my opinion, you need some browns, some dark yellows."

"I don't like them."

"You also need oil and turpentine, and also, of course, a palette."

"Are they expensive?"

"Here are some inexpensive ones. The box and palette, with two flasks, cost only twelve francs. See whether the palette is right for your hand."

He did not know how to use it, why there was a hole in it.

"Like that, you see? The hollow of the palette against your body, the curved part on the outside. It'll be easier when your hand gets bigger."

"How much does it all come to?"

He was radiant. He fingered the coins in his pocket. The salesman looked at each label, wrote down the figures, and added them up rapidly.

"Thirty-four francs and sixty centimes."

Louis would not have thought that such little tubes would cost so much. A big tube of blue was marked only two francs and contained ten times as much paint as the others. Without daring to ask for an explanation, he spluttered:

"I don't have enough money. I'll be back. Be sure to hold them for me. Until what time is the store open?"

"Seven o'clock."

The man must have thought he wouldn't come back, and there was a touch of melancholy in his eyes as he watched Louis walk out. However, when he saw him start running as soon as he reached the sidewalk, he smiled confidently. From there to Rue Mouffetard Louis slowed up a bit not more than twice, in order to catch his breath. His mother was still at her post.

"Mama!"

"What's the matter with you?"

"Nothing. Listen. It's very important. You've absolutely got to lend me fifteen francs. I swear I'll give it back to you."

"What do you intend to do with fifteen francs?"

"You'll see. I'll tell you later. I'm in a hurry."

She had never seen him like that. It was the first time he had ever manifested keen, insistent passion.

"Here! But don't knock yourself out like that."

He bought others, later on, from the same salesman, who had taken a liking to him. Neither knew the other's name, but there was a kind of secret bond between them.

"Someday you'll need an easel. What do you paint on?"

"On heavy paper."

"You'll have to try canvas."

He showed some prepared stretchers and explained the various sizes.

"After all, you can prepare the canvas yourself, with glue and zinc white. Lots of painters do."

He dared not believe it and yet he now lived only for that, as if the years before had been only a secret preparation. He painted near the window when he returned from work in the morning, for that was when the light was best.

If anyone had spoken to him about models, he would have been thoroughly surprised. He did not look at anything, except at times the workmen who made a din with their pickaxes demolishing the fronts of M. Stieb's shoe store and of the tripery next to it. Scaffolds were erected. The demolishers were followed by other workers, and one afternoon there came to life the smartest-looking store on the street, with two all-glass show windows and a glass entrance as well, and, inside, a big room furnished with mahogany armchairs and matching stools. There was a section for ladies at the left and for gentlemen at the right, and at the back one could see a dapple-gray rocking horse for children.

M. Stieb hired saleswomen, whom he picked young and pretty. Alice, who had gone back to work in the laundry, applied for a job in the shoe store and was taken on. It was indirectly because of M. Stieb, who dressed more and more elegantly, that she found a husband, for one afternoon she had to wait on a tall, dark, slightly awkward young man. The following day, he waited for her after work. They went dancing together on Saturdays. Three months later, Alice announced to her mother that she was getting married in the spring.

"His name is Gaston, Gaston Cottereau. He's twenty-five and works in a big delicatessen on Rue de Rennes. If only you could see what there is in the window! They make lobster in scallop shells, shrimp salad, chicken croquettes . . ."

"Where does he live?"

"For the time being, he rents a room in his boss's apartment, but we're looking for a place of our own in the neighborhood."

"What about François?"

"Gaston doesn't want me to work after we're married, and François will live with us."

François was a big, rosy, pug-nosed boy who resembled nobody in the family and who was already walking on his big chubby legs.

Louis hardly remembered the marriage or the wedding dinner on the first floor of a restaurant. Strangers were present, Gaston's parents, who lived at Saint-Aubin, in Nièvre. They had ruddy faces that looked as if they had been carved in wood.

He tried the next day and the following days to paint portraits of them sitting stiffly in front of the white tablecloth, and, without knowing why, he included the body of a woman lying on the cloth, a nude body resembling his sister's. The head was only a blurred outline, as if it were unimportant.

He was unsatisfied with what he painted, bcause it remained muddy. He refused to let himself mix colors and found it hard to place faces and objects on different planes.

There were schools. His salesman on Rue de Richelieu had asked him whether he would enter the School of Fine Arts when he was old enough, and Louis dared not admit to him that he had only his elementary school diploma and worked at Les Halles at night. He expected to work there all his life and to be promoted little by little, for M. Samuel liked him.

"Say, little one. Climb up the stepladder and try to write figures in the columns."

Louis did not know that the man who had been writing prices on the blackboard for years had entered the hospital the day before and probably would not come out alive. He was to undergo an operation the next day or the following day, though he did not know for what.

"I can't reach the top, sir."

"Write on the other lines."

Samuel called out a few figures to him at random. The chalk grated on the blackboard, the way it used to do in school. Louis followed tensely, as if his life depended on it.

"Your figures are better than poor Albert's. I can read them without my glasses. Let's see your handwriting. Here goes! Cauliflowers. Carrots. Turnips. Not so fast! Best quality peaches. Cavaillon melons. All right! You can come down. I'll tell Michel to raise the stepladder another foot. Starting Monday, I'll give you sixty francs a month and we'll see about a raise at the end of the year."

It was wonderful! He didn't tell his mother because he wanted to surprise her when she came to stock up. The neighborhood tradeswomen had recognized him.

"Gabrielle! Look up there . . ."

She waved to him in surprise, but he had no time to wave back. He was catching figures on the wing, rubbing out, writing, looking down at people's heads, which appeared to him in a different light.

His work thrilled him. The look of the shed changed every moment. He could have painted for ten years without exhausting the material he had before his eyes.

Alice and her husband had found a fourth-floor apartment on Rue des Ecoles, opposite the Sorbonne.

"We even have a balcony. So François can be out in the air when I do the housework."

She often walked with her son, holding him by the hand, to Rue Mouffetard and chatted with her mother, who would cram her shopping bag with vegetables, but she almost never went up to the apartment where she had lived so long.

There were only two of them in it now, and it was all the more comfortable in that they were hardly ever there at the same time, except on Sunday.

Louis found a secondhand bed, which he put against the wall, in Emilie's old place. He bought a night table with a cracked marble top which he got for a song.

When his mother's bed was pulled over to the night table, there remained a big empty space on the window side, and one day he set up an easel there, a light, cheap, deal easel for which he had been hankering a long time.

He had perhaps found a way of thinning his paint, of keeping it from being pasty, what he called smeary, though he was not sure of the result. Instead of spreading it carefully, as on a wall or door, he used a fine brush and dabbed touches of pure tones on the cardboard. For he continued to be haunted by pure colors. He never felt they were limpid enough, vibrant enough. He would have liked to see them quiver.

He was not yet ready to use canvas and found all the cardboard cartons he wanted on top of garbage cans. He prepared them as the salesman had advised him. It took a lot of time, but he had no sense of time. He had never had it; events that were years apart had no chronological order in his mind.

He was sleeping warmly and voluptuously one day when he felt someone touch his shoulder and then heard his mother's voice:

"Louis! Wake up!"

He was struck by the tone of it, for it was grave, tragic.

"What's the matter, Mama?"

She stared at him. She was pale and drawn and looked as if she had suddenly been frozen by fate.

"They've declared war, Louis."

"Where?"

"Here. In France. The Germans have attacked us. There are posters up announcing a general mobilization."

"Do you think the Germans'll get to Paris?"

"I hope we lick them. Men are leaving, regiments are parading . . ."

He had no reaction, and he thought he heard a tone of reproach in his mother's voice when she added:

"Vladimir will be among the first to go."

He hadn't thought of Vladimir. His first thought had been that he was only sixteen, that he was too short to be a soldier, and that since the Germans weren't near Paris life would continue as usual.

"If the twins are in France or in the colonies, they'll be mobilized too, because they're going on nineteen."

She was counting on her fingers and moving her lips.

"In fact they're over nineteen, since they were born in April. They'll be pulled in right away, and if they don't show up they'll be deserters."

"I'm sorry, Mama."

"It's only natural. And there's Alice's husband, who's in the cavalry of the line. They're the ones who ride out ahead of the lines. He once explained it to me without realizing it would soon be happening."

She bent over and kissed him listlessly, with her mind elsewhere.

"I wonder if Vladimir will come to say good-by to me."

He came in the evening, in service uniform, with his pack on his back. He seemed unimpressed by the events.

"Hello, Mama. Hello, you."

He kissed them on both cheeks.

"I've got to get going. Have to be at the East Station. This is no day for missing the train. See you both soon. Don't worry, we'll lick them!"

A blonde woman, heavily made up and wearing high heels, was waiting for him in the street and took his arm. Storekeepers brought him various things, one a cheese, another a half bottle of cognac, which he crammed into his pack.

The florist handed him a carnation, and Vladimir stuck it into the end of his rifle. When he disappeared at the foot of the street, Gabrielle left the window where she had been leaning her elbows and sat down at the table.

"Hand me the wine, will you, Louis?" she murmured.

That evening she got drunk alone, dismally drunk, while groups of young people paraded in the street screaming patriotic songs and drinking songs.

II

THE WAR LEFT few traces on Louis, some memories relating mainly to his family. No one at home had ever read the papers, nor did they now, since only he and his mother were left in the apartment. He tried to read them, because he heard people talk about communiqués. He tried again later, when he was older, but never managed to be interested in the news. It was just words and phrases that had no effect on him. He couldn't feel or smell or touch them. There was no vibration.

Perhaps if he had been four or five inches taller in 1914, he would have been swept up in the general frenzy and have volunteered without waiting to be called up. Then, in the trenches, the war would have entered him, would have been part of his being and, as must have been the case of so many others, would have accompanied him throughout his life.

On Rue Mouffetard, the frenzy, apart from some singing and a few bouts of drunkenness, was practically nonexistent. It was a street on which people's main concern was to get enough to eat every day, and, for those who had children, to feed them.

At Les Halles, one saw fewer and fewer young men, then middle-aged men started leaving, but the rhythm remained the same, cabbages remained cabbages, poultry was still poultry, and one continued to see sides of beef hanging from hooks and the little train from Arpajon waiting by the sheds.

He was to retain only a confused memory of historic dates, of battles whose names would be carved in stone, and he mixed up the names of the generals.

His first real memory of war, apart from the general mobilization, which he had experienced only from his window, was his sister's arrival one evening while his mother and he were having dinner together in the kitchen. Her eyes were red and dazed, and he thought her gestures theatrical. She had rushed from the doorway straight to her mother, who had had just time enough to catch her in her arms.

"Mama! Oh, Mama! It's awful . . ."

It was false. His sister wasn't like that. His mother had also, on the first day, adopted a tragic attitude that didn't become her. Both of them were perhaps sincere, but they exaggerated their gestures, like people who made speeches.

Alice sobbed on a bosom where he had never seen her lay her head, and she sobbed without speaking. Finally she pulled away and held out an official-looking paper.

"It's to inform me that Gaston's dead. He was killed in a forest near Charleroi, in Belgium, while he was on patrol."

To Louis, this Gaston Cottereau was a stranger, and had he lived he would have remained on the fringes of the family, just like young François, who was his sister's son but did not resemble any of them physically.

He nevertheless became conscious that evening that war really killed. For him, this was the first casualty.

"My poor child! You married at the wrong time, but there was no way of knowing, nobody could have known. Where's François?"

"I left him with a neighbor, a woman whose husband's also at the front."

"What are you going to do?"

"I don't know yet. It seems we'll be given help, a pension. We'd hardly finished setting up the apartment."

Then she became aware of her brother's presence.

"You, Louis, you're lucky!"

She had no need to be more precise. She was alluding not to his age but his shortness. He did not remain present at the whining of the two women, who were hardly sincere, in any case not Gabrielle, who had never liked either Gaston or his family.

He left for work. In Samuel's shed nothing had changed, except that an office clerk and two stock clerks had left and been replaced.

His colors, as he said, for he never uttered the word "paint," remained his basic concern. The war was reflected in his work in the form of flags, bugles gleaming in the sun, soldiers in red trousers, shoulder braid. Later, when the uniforms were changed, he liked the blue, which he put into several pictures.

His sister did not stay in Paris long. Gaston's parents, still remembering perhaps the Franco-Prussian War of 1870, imagined that the capital was starving and the Parisians were eating rats. They had written to Alice from their village in Nièvre asking her to come to Saint-Aubin, where they had a farm and three or four cows and where the child would be sure of being properly fed.

"I've found someone who'll rent my apartment, the wife of an English officer who has some post or other in Paris."

After a little more than a year, Louis moved to the glass cage, for another employee had been mobilized. He was earning a hundred francs a month. His mother too was taking in more money than before the war, and they felt almost rich.

As their occupations obliged them to play hide-and-seek and one couldn't light a fire in midsummer just to prepare coffee or fry two eggs, they had a gas ring installed next to the old stove, which of course would be used in winter, and after a few weeks they were so used to it that they couldn't understand how they had ever been able to do without it.

When they had dinner together, Gabrielle would sometimes fall into a melancholy reverie. It was not the violent, spectacular grief of the early days, but it was more impressive.

"Vladimir doesn't write to us. Just two little notes, simply to say that he's well and that he's been made a corporal. I'm sure he writes to that girl, who he never bothered to introduce to us and whose name we don't even know."

Nor did they know what Vladimir had lived on between the end of his military service and the declaration of war. When he returned from his long stay in Toulon, he was a different man. He was tanned, had new mannerisms, and made gestures he had never made before, and he looked more aggressive than ever.

"Are you going back to work for M. Brillanceau? I met him two months ago, and he's ready to take you on again."

"He's likely to wait a long time."

His smile was derisive. He had always been derisive, but not in that casual way.

"What do you expect to do?"

"I don't know. I've rented a room and I'll see what comes up."

He made no mention of the possibility of living at home again.

"You'll stay in the neighborhood at least?"

"I've seen enough of the neighborhood. I'm going to live on Rue de Clichy."

She was timid in his presence, as if she were afraid he would get angry and go away for good.

"Will you come to see us?"

"Of course."

"Will you leave me your address?"

"When it's definite, I'll let you know. For the time being, I'm living in a hotel."

"Isn't it very expensive?"

"I manage."

All the same, he had dropped in for a moment to kiss her before leaving for the front, but not without accompanying the girl who was waiting for him on the sidewalk.

Two brief notes in more than a year! He must have had furloughs, like the others, and he had certainly been in Paris.

Of course, the family was not in the habit of being effusive, and Gabrielle had led her life in her own way without bothering much about the children as soon as they were old enough to stand on their hind legs.

Louis discovered little by little that the bonds between Gabrielle and her children were stronger than he had thought. Her attitude did not resemble the mother love that he heard people talk about or that one learned about in school.

It was rather as if, without her realizing it, the umbilical cord that had connected her with her children had never been completely cut.

"It's funny, Louis, that you've started to paint."

She rarely spoke to him about his pictures. He was sure she glanced at them when she got home, but they bore so little resemblance to her idea of what a painting was that she preferred to say nothing.

"Are you planning to make it your profession?"

"It's not a profession."

"There are some people who make a living at it. I used to know an old fellow who wore a big hat and a polka-dot four-in-hand. He was a specialist.

"If I remember right, that was before you were born. I wasn't bad-looking in those days. He claimed I was beautiful, that I could earn my living as a model just by lying naked and not moving.

"I once went to pose for him in his studio near Saint-

Germain-des-Prés, and he didn't even touch me. He hardly talked to me. I felt like laughing all the time, I don't know why. It seemed funny to me to be all naked for hours in front of a gentleman who didn't try to paw me. He gave me five francs and told me to come back whenever I wanted. He made a good living and had, in addition to the studio, a nice apartment, well furnished, with a big balcony."

She felt like adding: "You ought to paint like him."

He was already doing better work with his touches of pure colors, especially since he had begun painting on canvas. The difficulty was still to make things that seemed to have no relationship "hang together."

He did not try to copy reality, a chair, a street, a woman, a streetcar, except as an occasional exercise, and he succeeded fairly well. But that was a mere matter of images. What he would have liked to get down on canvas was reality itself, as he saw it, or rather as it composed itself spontaneously in his mind.

For example, he had put little François in the middle of the schoolyard, alone, unsteady on his chubby legs. It was a winter scene, since there was snow, but he wanted the sky to be a summer sky, and a red and yellow streetcar, full of faces pressed against the windows, was going by in front of the wall.

He could not have explained. It was too complicated. The salesman in the store on Rue de Richelieu had urged him so often that he finally went to Rue du Faubourg-Saint-Honoré and Rue La Boétie where there were several picture galleries.

"You'll see the best Impressionists, Cézanne, Renoir, Sisley, Pissarro. Not long ago, people made fun of them, and now you've got to be very rich to buy one of their paintings. You'll also see the Fauves, Vlaminck, Derain, and others whose names I've forgotten. One of them's an odd type, a half-tramp, who spends his life in the Montmartre saloons. You can recognize his paintings a mile away."

He had looked at the canvases exhibited in the windows

and was annoyed with himself because they left him cold. They were good, of course. He felt crushed by the craftsmanship of those painters who knew where to put their spots of color and how to give them their full value.

He was nevertheless disappointed. What he saw did not resemble what he was looking for. If he showed his paintings to the salesman, the latter would lose interest in him. Louis had finally learned his name because he had heard someone call him from the back of the shop: M. Suard. He was a friend of a painter named Marquet and of another one who was younger, Othon Friesz.

"Some of them come from quite a distance to get their supplies in our store because we have foreign brands, especially Dutch, which are hard to find in Paris."

"Are they pure?"

"In my opinion, they fade less rapidly. The trouble with most paints is that they start getting dark, and present-day painters don't want to varnish their work. Besides, how can you varnish paint that's laid on thick?"

He was learning words, unsuspected techniques.

"Haven't you ever been tempted to work in a studio, Julian's, for example? They have good models and a teacher who gives advice."

M. Suard was as delighted by Louis's naïveté about painting as by his passion.

"It's not a matter of schools, like the Fine Arts. You go whenever you like. You bring your materials, set yourself up in front of an easel that's not being used, and you draw or paint the model. You pay by the hour."

Louis had almost asked: "What model?"

But remembering his mother and the painter with the big hat who specialized in peddlers, he had understood.

"There's a studio not far from here, on Rue du Faubourg-Montmartre."

He had gone there one morning with his box. The light was

as cold as at certain hours in M. Samuel's shed, except that you never saw the light, because the place had a northern exposure. The silence was impressive, sinister. Thirty or forty people, men and women, especially girls and middle-aged men, stood or sat in front of easels around a wooden stand on which a naked girl with skinny thighs stood with her hands clasped at the back of her neck.

Some were painting, others drawing, erasing, drawing again, while an old gentleman with pince-nez and a goatee planted himself silently behind each in turn.

Occasionally he would point, without saying a word, to a charcoal stroke. Or else he would grab a girl's brush and with two or three touches correct the movement of an arm or position of a leg.

"Do you want an easel?"

"No, sir. Thank you."

He could not have worked in that atmosphere and had no need of the model. Someday perhaps, if he had the courage, he would talk to M. Suard about what he had in mind, but it was impossible to explain if it wasn't down on canvas.

When he finished a picture, he would, in most cases, scrape it down with a palette knife, a smooth, flexible instrument that was voluptuous to handle. After a few days of drying, he would spread a layer of zinc white and so have a new canvas, which saved him money.

"Louis, I wonder what's become of the twins."

He too thought back to the past every now and then. At times he would conjure up the image of Emilie, of whom no one had spoken for years. His mother had precise memories about each of them, but they were not the same as his, so that when they had these conversations they did not echo each other.

"Do you remember the day when a distinguished-looking gentleman with a decoration in his lapel came in with Olivier in his arms? Olivier was unconscious. Guy and he had been playing. They'd been jumping over a bench with their feet together.

Olivier missed and his head hit the pavement so hard that the gentleman, who was reading on the same bench and who might very well have been annoyed with them for disturbing him, thought he was dead."

"Was I born then?"

"I think so. Of course! Am I dumb! You must have been at least six, since you were going to school."

He had no recollection of the incident, any more than his mother remembered most of the events that, for him, constituted the history of the family.

"The thing that consoles me is knowing they weren't unhappy."

He would look at her without understanding, disturbed at the fact that other memories were being mixed with his, for he no longer felt so sure of himself. They were like false notes.

"Have you forgotten that they ran away a first time and were found in a freight train, in Rouen?"

"I remember . . ."

"If the police chief . . ."

He would listen abstractedly, irritated, unwilling to hear all the details again.

"The second time . . ."

"I know, Mama."

She would glance at him reproachfully.

"I had to see a doctor last week because I had pains in my stomach. I didn't say anything to you about it so as not to worry you and because it was a woman's thing."

He had heard allusions to venereal diseases and wondered whether his mother had one, which made him blush.

"It's unimportant. He was a very nice man, very understanding. He asked me questions about my life. I told him about the twins and admitted that what happened must have been my fault.

"He swore it wasn't, that neither I nor the kind of life we led had caused them to run away. Doctors know all about that kind of thing, and now I understand why the chief was a little lenient with them.

"It's in their blood. They take after their father, who didn't get along anywhere and who ended up you know how.

"I'm sure those two were Heurteau's. I've every reason to think so. About Alice, I couldn't swear, but I'd rather she weren't."

He was obliged to sit and listen. It made him uncomfortable. He was interested, of course, but he would have preferred that she not speak of such things.

"There are kids who run away five or six times a year. Even when they're locked up, they find a way of getting out and some get killed trying to escape by the window, like sleepwalkers. Did you know that?"

"No."

"The thing that reassures me is that in most cases they get over it when they're older. It gives me hope of seeing them someday. Don't forget they're over twenty. They ought to be in the army. I wonder why we've never got a notice from their draft board."

"You know, Mama, all the red tape . . ."

"All the same, it's funny. When it comes to military service, they usually know how to find people. They have enough military police for that!"

That must have been in 1916. The war had been going on for two years and people were no longer surprised.

Had Gabrielle had a premonition? A few days after that conversation, she received an official paper, as had Alice two years before, informing her that her son, Sergeant Olivier Heurteau, had been killed in front of Fort Douaumont in the course of a dangerous operation for which he had volunteered and that he had been awarded the distinguished-service medal post-humously.

The personal effects that had been found on him would be sent to the family later.

What intrigued both of them was that the African Battalions had a bad reputation, or at least had had before the war, for they were composed of troublemakers, delinquents, pimps from the Porte Saint-Martin district, Montmartre and elsewhere, of boys who had been in reformatories and those who had had a police record before the age for military service.

It was also odd to have news of only one of the redheads, and Gabrielle would not have been surprised to learn that they had died at the same time.

Olivier's personal effects arrived shortly thereafter. He had been the leader of the pair, the one who looked older, whereas Guy, who was as tall as his twin and had the same build, seemed milder, hesitant, and followed his brother around like a shadow.

Gabrielle and Louis learned from the service certificate that Olivier had volunteered for the African Battalions long before the war, with his "parents' consent," from which they inferred that he had faked his mother's handwriting.

His address was given as Rue d'Oran and his occupation as that of agriculturist. His effects included a switchblade knife with a horn handle. The blade had been sharpened often and he must have used it in North Africa and in the trenches. An old wallet, which had lain in the mud, contained only a few bank notes, some postage stamps—why stamps, since soldiers' letters were post free?—a postcard from Algeria to an address written in an almost illegible handwriting and signed with a name that was undecipherable. Above the signature were drawn a star, a heart, and an animal that could have been a goat as well as a horse.

A blurred photograph was perhaps the key to this message, for it showed a young Bedouin woman squatting on the ground next to a donkey that was loaded with two baskets.

She looked about thirteen or fourteen and had a tattoo mark in the middle of her forehead, unless it was only a stain on the print. Her big gaping eyes were looking straight ahead with an expression of adoration.

"Don't you think she's his girl friend?"

"I don't know, Mama."

"I don't think they're allowed to marry there while they're still in the army, especially with a native woman. Besides, if he were married, she's the one they'd have sent his things to."

The remaining items were a pipe, a pig-bladder pouch in which there was still a little tobacco, and a tinder pipe-lighter.

"Guy must have joined up the same time as he, in the same regiment. I'm going to inquire at the War Department. I'll go myself, because if I write to them they won't answer."

She spent a whole day there, not only at headquarters, but in the offices scattered all over Paris. When she got home, she was in a state of exhaustion but was still hopeful.

"I'll find the right door sooner or later. I've never seen so many women, young and old, waiting in line in yards and hallways. A lieutenant, who resembles the police chief, promised me that within a week he'd have the list of those who volunteered for the African Battalions in 1912."

She smiled, and there was a certain pride in her expression.

"You know, Louis, it was wrong of us to think there are only roughnecks in the African Battalions. I asked the lieutenant. He agreed that they were made up mainly of troublemakers and boys who'd been sentenced.

"But it's different in the case of those who sign up, boys attracted by adventure and a hard life around the desert and who sleep in a tent more often than in a barrack room. He said to me, 'At the front, they're our best soldiers.' He knew one personally who'd become a second lieutenant and after ten years of service became a priest."

She did get a reply, not after a week but after about a month. It was brought by an orderly, as if mail from the Ministries was too important or confidential to be entrusted to the post office. The letter confirmed the fact that Olivier Heurteau had enlisted as a volunteer on October 21, 1912, but stated that there was no record of a Guy Heurteau in the African regiments for that year or the following years.

"Do you think that means he's dead?"

"I don't know, Mama. They might have separated. Maybe Guy fell in love with a girl and married her."

"He couldn't have done that without my consent. He wasn't of age."

"Olivier couldn't join up either. Maybe Guy went to live in another country, in South America, for example. When he lived here, he often talked about South America."

She shook her head skeptically. It remained a mystery to her, and Louis could tell from certain silences and a certain vague look that would suddenly come over her face that the matter preyed on her mind.

Louis was becoming more and more friendly with M. Suard, and he would sometimes drop into the stationery store on Rue de Richelieu when he saw that the salesman was not busy, just to chat with him, without buying a tube of paint.

"It's too bad I married so young and had children right away. I have three, one of them a girl your age.

"And even so, I'm glad she's a girl. Otherwise the draft board would soon be after her!

"Remember, I'm not complaining. I myself once dreamed of being a painter. That's why I asked to be assigned to this department.

"Later, who knows, I may even become a picture dealer, I may open a small gallery. Not with big names, because that requires too much capital and there's no merit in it. With young painters that I discover. I already have a few canvases that some customers let me have cheap . . ."

Was it out of graciousness, so as not to disturb Louis, that he added:

"When you're satisfied with what you're doing, I'd be glad to see one of your paintings."

"I'll never be satisfied. You know well enough that I'm not a real painter."

At the beginning of 1917—in any case, it was the winter when it was so cold and there was a shortage of coal, the winter too when there was talk of mutiny of troops and soldiers' being shot as an example—at the beginning of 1917, Gabrielle learned from a peddler on Rue Saint-Antoine who had formerly worked on Rue Mouffetard that Vladimir was in Paris.

The woman claimed she had seen him on the boulevard, not far from Rue Montmartre, where she had gone to visit her daughter who was a saleswoman.

"I swear to you, Gabrielle, I wasn't mistaken. Don't forget that I knew him when he was a tot and that later he used to swipe peaches from my cart. He was wearing a marine's uniform, with a beret, and he had a bandage on his head. People turned around to look at him and he seemed proud of it. I yelled out to him, 'Hey! Vladimir! Don't you recognize your friends any more?' And he yelled back, 'Hello, Aunt Emma!' That's what he used to call me when you and I were always together, with our carts side by side."

"And to think he didn't come to see me!"

"If he was wounded, he's on sick leave. He has all the time in the world."

"Meanwhile he's living at that awful woman's place."

"It's just as if he were married."

"You're right. I'm getting jealous of my children. His sister hasn't written us once in the last two months and we've received only a photograph of her son."

Vladimir came and even presented his mother with an oriental jewel, a charm that probably was not made of gold but that she thereafter wore proudly on her neck. He spoke of the Balkans, of Constantinople, as if he were talking about Clignancourt or the Porte des Lilas.

"Have you heard that Olivier's dead?"

"No."

"He was a sergeant and got the distinguished-service medal. I have it here. Do you want to see it?"

"I've seen so many of them! What about Guy? Dead too?"

"We have no news of Guy. Nobody knows what's become of him."

He could have said of the dead what he had just said of distinguished-service medals: he had seen so many!

"What about you, with your wound, didn't they give you a decoration?"

Louis shuddered when he saw his brother's face and heard the sound of his cutting voice:

"I'm not the kind of guy they give medals to. Even if I were dead, like Olivier."

"Don't you want to let me have your address in Paris, in case I have news of Guy?"

He merely answered evasively:

"I'll be back to see you before I leave."

"When are you going?"

"When the medicos decide."

"Is it serious?"

"A hole in the skull. They removed what they could, but there's still a piece of shrapnel somewhere."

"Do you still have pain?"

"Occasionally."

One afternoon by pure chance, Louis ran into an old acquaintance on the Pont Saint-Michel: the huge, colossal M. Pliska, who now had a beard and whose blond hair flowed down the back of his neck. Louis would not have been sure it was he if the Czech giant had not recognized him and crushed his hand.

"Little Louis, eh? What happening?"

His French was hardly better than in the past, and he still

accompanied his words with gesticulations and questioning looks.

"Your mother, Gabrielle? Gabrielle, yes?"

He remembered the pretty redhead with whom he had lived for almost two months, but he was no longer sure of her name.

"Brother Vladimir. Little sister. Big girl now?"

"She's married and has a son."

"Me, very hard, lots trouble, because me foreigner. Two years in camp concen . . . how you say? Hard word. Concentra . . ."

"Concentration."

"In nice country. Sun. South France, but pointy wire."

"Barbed wire."

"Yes. Huts bad. Soup bad. Lots little bugs. Fleas, you say? And in hair?"

"Lice?"

"Everybody lice. Now over. Me, studio. Come see studio. Heavy work. Sculpture. Dealers come see sculpture. Not buy, but come see."

Louis went with him as much out of curiosity as out of fear of offending him. They went by trolley to Boulevard Montparnasse. Pliska took him to Rue Campagne-Première, where they entered a rather recently built house.

"Here. Elevator. You know?"

There was indeed an elevator, which carried them to the top floor, the sixth, where Pliska took out a key and proudly opened his door.

"My studio."

Louis was dazzled. The room was vast and was flooded with light that streamed in through a huge window that separated it from the street. Part of the slanted roof was also glazed.

"Magnificent, is no? Me work."

He took off his jacket, vest, and tie with the air of a wrestler challenging spectators from the platform of a fair booth.

Louis's gaze was attracted by a big block of clay on a rotating pedestal in the middle of the room.

"See? When finished, terrific. Terrific one says?"

For the time being, it suggested a couple locked in embrace. Louis could recognize human shapes, but without being able to tell what was a leg or an arm. He was moved. He looked at it eagerly and was filled with a sweet feeling. There was, in particular, a rather heavy mass, a rump which was already definitely modeled and which gave him a deeper impression of sensuality than the rump of a live woman.

"To sculpt very hard. Very much hard. Here . . ."

On a plain wooden slab stood a horse and rider made of bits of iron that looked as if they had been picked up in a workshop.

"Don Quisote."

"Don Quixote?"

"Yes. Funny. No. Not funny."

He frowned. His limpid eyes clouded over.

"Dealers say funny. Me not funny. Me and dealers . . ."

He made a show of throwing them through the glass and into the street from his top floor.

"Much work. Much make love. Not much eat because not sell. So me carry beef."

"At Les Halles?"

"Halles, yes. Know Halles?"

When he learned that Louis worked there too, he wanted to have a drink with him and opened a bottle whose shape and label recalled an old Christmas.

"Not drink?"

"No. Too young."

"Me, drink too much. Not good."

He beat his chest like a gorilla and burst out laughing.

"See you Halles. You come back. You see love finished."

What he called love was the half-ton block of clay in the middle of the studio. Although they worked so near each other at night, it was a long time before they met again, for Les Halles had sharply defined areas and varied activities, and Pliska's working hours, for example, did not coincide with Louis's.

On being promoted and getting an increase, Louis had locked himself up in a glass cage and could no longer, as in the beginning, thread his way through the market carrying messages from M. Samuel to the agents on the neighboring streets or in the big sheds.

It was unquestionably as a result of his meeting with the Czech that the idea of a studio took root in him, and from then on, when he walked in the street, he would make sure whether or not there was a big glass window or, better still, a workshop at the back of a yard.

His turn came to receive an official paper. He had to report to the district office on March 12th with a copy of his birth certificate and appear before the draft board. He did not mention it to his mother, who had been out when he found the envelope under the door. He spent an anxious week, not in fear of being declared fit for service, but at the thought that he would have to appear naked in front of men.

He was the only one in the family who was modest. His mother and sister were not at all ashamed of their nakedness, which they exhibited with a casualness that was perhaps not unmingled with satisfaction. Vladimir had begun to hide his sex organs only when he was about thirteen, and as for the redheads, they had paid no attention to them at all.

Louis had never moved his bowels in the pot, except in very early childhood, of which he had no memory.

Even though it was freezing cold on the stairs in winter, even though it was menacingly dark, just as it was in the yard, he nevertheless would go down at night when he would start feeling sick as a result of holding it in.

And when he was bathed in the tub, he always held a wash-

cloth with which he hid his genitals as long as he was not sheltered by the soapy water.

There were at least forty of them gathered in a dusty room.
There were no clothes hooks, but they were nonetheless ordered to undress.

"Be quick about it, boys. Another batch is due at eleven."

He was more embarrassed when he recognized former
schoolmates, three or four of them, including the lawyer's son
whose name he had forgotten, the one who had left the public
school to enter a private one.

"Well, well!" he exclaimed. "The little saint!"

A wiseacre called out, after looking Louis up and down:

"Are you sure it's not a girl?"

"We used to take him for a boy, but he's had time to change.
Let's see your tool, little saint, so we can tell what you really
are."

Covering himself with his hands, he tried to turn his back to
them.

"He'll have to show it when he goes by. And you know what
the medical officer's going to do? He'll yank your balls and if
he doesn't like you, he'll stick a finger up your behind. Don't
think I'm making it up. My brother was called up last year
and tipped me off. Why do they call you the little saint? Do you
go to confession every morning? You want to stay a virgin till
you're married?"

The door finally opened into a larger room where men were
sitting at a table covered with a green cloth. He could not distinguish them from each other. Although he did not shut his
eyes, he saw only shadows, silhouettes, two horizon-blue uniforms, and a line of naked bodies.

"Step up. Stand up straight. Straighter than that. What are
your hands fiddling with?"

One of the men in uniform announced:

"Five feet, three quarters of an inch."

146

There was a roar of laughter.

"Come here," ordered the doctor.

Perhaps at the rate men were being consumed at the front, height no longer mattered? He was not afraid of being hit by a bullet, of being killed by a shell. What frightened him was the brutality, the orders that were rapped out in a snarling voice, the obligation to do what was ordered, without discussion.

He had made up his mind that if he were given a gun he would never fire it, or fire only in the air.

The medical officer dug his fingers between Louis's ribs, between his shoulder blades, then, after feeling his muscles, declared:

"Unfit. Rejected."

He was pushed out of the room.

"What are you waiting for, my boy? Didn't you hear the doctor? The country doesn't want you."

He let three days go by before saying to his mother, at dinner, in an expressionless tone:

"You know, Mama, I've been rejected."

"That's no misfortune. That way, I'm sure of having one of you."

Louis looked at her with the vague smile that intrigued them all and that did not necessarily reflect joy or gaiety.

His war was over.

III

HIS MOTHER CONTINUED going to Les Halles every morning to stock up, but she was less often heard joking aloud in her clear, vibrant voice. He remembered the time when he would recognize its brightness amidst the hubbub in the glass-roofed warehouse, as one recognized from a distance the brightness of her hair.

His grandmother too continued pushing her cart through the dark streets in the early hours of the morning, but there were more and more days when she did not turn up and when Gabrielle, between clients, would go up to her room at the foot of the street, near Saint Médard's Church, to make sure she wasn't sick and didn't need anything.

Louis hardly knew that room. He had been in it two or three times, when he was little, and remembered it as being dark and crowded with furniture. There was a dining-room buffet through whose upper doors, which were made of glass, he could see crockery. There were a table and chairs with fake-antique carvings, greenish velvet curtains with satin-stitch embroidery, and also knickknacks, vases, statuettes, porcelain candy dishes.

"Be careful, Louis. The last time your brother Vladimir came, he broke another saucer that I was very fond of. They're souvenirs."

The smell of the room was different from the one at home, and he suspected the old woman of not liking to have visitors, not even her grandchildren. He had always considered her old, but she was not so very old, for the girls in the family had children early.

In the spring of 1919 Gabrielle must have been fifty-four. Her brother, the butcher, whom they pretended to ignore, though his store was on their street, and who ignored them too, did not know that Louis was his nephew. He had been the old lady's first child. She had had him when she was about sixteen.

She had grown very thin and was becoming cranky. Once, when she had not turned up at Les Halles for a whole week, Gabrielle reassured Louis, who was worried.

"Don't be upset about Grandma. She could live on her savings. She's put aside quite a pile. She's never spent a penny. And she didn't help me in the beginning either, even when I was in a tight spot. She'd say to me, 'Every man for himself! One brings up one's children until they're old enough to manage. After that, they can fend for themselves. I don't expect anything from anyone, and I have no desire when I'm old to sue you and your brother to make you give me an allowance.' "

It was between eight and nine in the evening. Louis and his mother were both at home.

"What do you feel like eating, Louis? An omelette? A steak?"

"An omelette, Mama, with cheese, if there is any."

They would sit at the table facing one another, and there would be long silences. One would have thought they were observing each other. Actually they were, or at least Louis was.

For years he had been seeing his mother with the same eyes, and she had always seemed to be the same age. Though she had hardly changed physically, for her body was still firm and her face unlined, he had the impression that a kind of grayness had invaded her.

In the past, she had never looked sad or preoccupied, and even the death of Emilie had dampened her spirits for only a few days. All in all, she had taken things as they came, enjoying what was good in life, contenting herself uncomplainingly with what was less good and ignoring the rest as if it had not existed.

Was it because her children were growing up and seeing her with new eyes that she had suddenly stopped receiving men? Yet she was still having them up when Vladimir was fifteen.

Her life had dimmed. To talk in terms of painting, like M. Suard, shade was forming, dull spots on the canvas.

When Louis took her out from time to time on Saturday night, she no longer wore the lavender-blue dress which he had been so fond of. Fashion had changed with the war. Petticoats had little by little disappeared, as had heavy boned corsets, dresses that swept the ground, and shoes that were laced halfway up the leg.

Women displayed not only their ankles but half of their calves and wore military-style jackets above their skirts. This caused so little astonishment that Louis had to make an effort to remember prewar fashions.

She still undressed in his presence.

"You don't mind my going out?"

"Why, Mama?"

"You may think I'm too old."

"You'll never be old."

"Doesn't it bother you to see your mother running to dance halls like a bitch in heat?"

He smiled at her in a way that was meant to be reassuring.

"You, you never go out."

"I go out during the day."

"I've never seen you with a girl friend. Do you have one?"

"No, Mama."

"Why not? A boy of nineteen needs women."

He realized what was worrying her, and it reminded him of the jokes in the office of the draft board.

"Don't be afraid. I'm a man."

She had not lost the habit of coming straight to the point.

"Do you do it?"

"Sometimes."

"You could have it for nothing, as much as you want, especially as most men are at the front. If only you knew how women squabble over soldiers on leave!"

"It would take up too much of my time."

That was not quite true, it expressed only part of a truth which was too complicated, which he was not sure he understood.

The memory of his impotence at the sight of a tangle of black hair had kept him for a long time from trying again. His appetite rarely had a keen enough edge to awaken his torment.

Erotic fantasies sometimes prevented him from falling asleep, as they did everyone, but he had found a method of making the physical need less acute. He made an effort at times to compose extravagant images, to see them as street scenes, as spots of color, to surround them with other details, and to create in his mind a picture of which he could have reproduced every detail.

There was a picture which he had a desire to paint but which he could not work on at the time because his mother would see it and he was ashamed of it.

Its colors would be as gay and bright as those he ordinarily used and yet, in advance, he entitled the composition "War."

He would start on it as soon as he had a studio, especially since the picture would be rather big. The vista would be that of the Champs-Elysées, with the greenery of the rows of trees and with bright houses whose details need not be visible, except for a profusion of flags at the windows.

The crowd would be represented by black spots dotted with blue, white, and red.

The important thing was the parade. As for the title, he hesitated between "War" and "The Parade," waiting for the canvas to be painted before deciding.

Ranks of soldiers, bigger than the crowd. He did not mind disproportion in his works among the figures or objects.

Naked soldiers, some of them rosy, others ghastly pale, as at the draft board. Each of them would carry a rifle and a peaked cap or helmet—he didn't know yet.

An officer, also naked, resembling the doctor, would be caracoling on a horse in front of them. They would be marching toward the Arch of Triumph, except that it would be replaced by the dark and monumental sex organ of a woman whose legs were spread.

It would be hard to achieve. He probably would never be able to bring it off. Yet he had succeeded with a painting almost as complicated which he called "The Little Train from Arpajon" and which, in his mind, was meant to epitomize Les Halles.

He had spoken about "The Little Train from Arpajon" to M. Suard, who said he would like to see the painting.

"As soon as I find a studio."

"There are some available ones in Montmartre."

"That's too far away."

Too far away from his mother, of course, for he would go to see his mother every day, most likely would have dinner with her. He did not know how the matter could be arranged, and he foresaw that it would be painful. The actual reason for his rejection of Montmartre was that he would feel he was in a foreign country there, far away from the images he had been collecting unwittingly for nineteen years.

When he left the stationery store one warm, humid afternoon, he had happened to pass a woman, not very tall, not young either, but plump, and with a pretty, smiling face. She had looked at him with complicity as she went by. The look was unlike that of the women who accosted men in the street. He had wondered whether he had quite understood. When he had looked back, she had too, the very same instant, and he had turned around and gone up to her.

She was wearing a blue suit with gilt buttons, and an overseas cap of the same color, which was in fashion at the moment, was set on her curly hair.

She had not waited for him to make the first advances.

"Will you come along with me? I live only five minutes away."

He warned her honestly that he was not rich.

"That doesn't matter. We'll arrange things."

She looked to him about thirty. One could have taken her for a saleswoman in a store on the Main Boulevards, or for a typist. She slightly resembled Mlle. Blanche, who worked with him every night in the glass cage and to whom he had never dared make a proposition, despite his desire to.

She lived in a cozy apartment on a street that ran along the Palais Royal, behind the Comédie Française. At the window, a canary was hopping about in a cage. The furniture and waxed floor were clean and bright.

"Do you often pick up women in the street?"

"It's the first time."

Or almost the first. The other one had called to him and all he had had to do was follow her.

"How old are you? Sixteen? Seventeen?"

"Nineteen. People think I'm younger because of my height."

"And because of your pretty little monkey face, eh? Do you know you've got a roguish look?"

She had taken off her hat and was undressing. Through an open door he could see a small dining room beyond which must have been a kitchen.

"Are you embarrassed?"

"I don't know. A little."

"Haven't you ever undressed in front of a woman?"

"Not entirely, no."

"Haven't you ever made love?"

She understood his silence.

"It's nothing to be ashamed of, you know. Everyone has had to start someday. At your age, it was the same with me. I finally made up my mind. I was pretty scared and you'd be amazed if you knew what I imagined it would be like."

She had thus far uncovered only her bosom, which was as beautiful as Gabrielle's, except that it did not have his mother's pearly sheen.

"Come and sit here."

He sat down beside her on a couch with a yellow cover that later appeared often in his paintings.

"Do you like breasts?"

"Yes, I do."

"Is that what excites you in a woman?"

She was speaking to him amiably, as if they were good friends who had known each other a long time.

"Don't think I'm in the habit of walking the streets. It looks like it, but it's very different. Haven't you ever been to what's called a massage establishment in the newspaper ads? Most of the time they're apartments.

"I'm at Mme. Georgette's on Rue Notre-Dame-de-Lorette. It's quiet and discreet. There are only three or four of us, rarely five, and the customers are well behaved. They visit us regularly. You ought to drop in. One of the girls, Arlette, is just twenty-one."

He stroked her breasts while looking at the canary in the cage, and she did not rush him. She kept talking casually. She unbuttoned his clothes little by little and he did not feel ashamed of being naked with her on the couch.

He wondered whether he wasn't going to love her. Entering her was an experience unlike what he had imagined. It was very smooth and a feeling of well-being flowed through his whole body.

"Stay like that for a moment," she whispered to him, stroking his hair and looking into his face with tender curiosity.

He was surprised, afterwards, that she did not act as if it were over, and they remained lying side by side, looking up at the ceiling and chatting.

"What do you do? I bet you're a student."

"I work at Les Halles."

"You? At Les Halles?"

"Someday I'll be a painter. I've started, but my work is bad."

Later, she did not get dressed but put on a bathrobe of the same blue as his mother's old dress.

He anxiously slipped his hand into his pocket, frightened at the thought that he might have to run home to get money as he had had to do the first time he bought paints.

"No. Not today. I've got another idea. Go down to the bakery. It's at the left, on Rue des Petits-Champs. Buy some cakes, whatever you like, except chocolate cake, because chocolate doesn't agree with me. There's a grocery opposite and if you have enough money left get a bottle of port. There's no point in buying the most expensive, because I wouldn't know the difference. To me, port is port."

Did she wonder whether he would come back or did she trust him? He read the names of the streets on the blue signs, for he was not familiar with the neighborhood. She lived on Rue Montpensier, and in order to get to Rue des Petits-Champs he had to go by way of Rue de Beaujolais.

He found the bakery and the grocery. Her odor was still on his skin, and it seemed to him that the passers-by could tell that he had made love twice.

She was leaning on the window sill with her elbows, near the canary, when he returned with his packages, and the door opened the moment he reached the landing.

"You're very nice."

Oddly enough, her name was Louise and his Louis.

"At Mme. Georgette's, they call me Loulou."

"May I call you Louise?"

"Would you rather? They say it sounds romantic, because of an opera."

"My name is Louis."

"Louis what?"

"Cuchas."

"Is it a foreign name?"

"I don't think so. It's my mother's and grandmother's name, and they were both born, just as I was, on Rue Mouffetard."

"Uncork the bottle. There's a corkscrew in the buffet."

They had gone into the dining room. The sky above the roofs of the Palais Royal was lovely, very gentle, in spite of the heat.

She filled the glasses and handed him one, and he looked into her eyes as he drank. He did not like liquor of any kind. It immediately made him dizzy.

"May I come back?"

"You seem to have liked it."

"I did. I . . ."

He was at a loss for words, he felt moved, was filled with a sentiment he had had only for his mother or sister and once or twice, when they were younger, for Vladimir. He would have liked her to remain happy and gay, he hoped nothing unpleasant would happen to her.

She refilled the glasses.

"Here's to you!"

He rather liked the taste, as he did the warmth he felt in his chest and then, later, in his head. His eyes must have been shining and his ears getting red.

"You know . . ."

"A little while ago you called me Louise . . ."

"You know, Louise . . ."

It was really too difficult to thank her as he would have liked, as she deserved, to make her understand the importance of what had just happened, of the wonderful gift she had just made him and which would last all his life, he was sure it would.

There was no way of her guessing it. He would also have liked to tell her that Mme. Georgette's didn't matter to him, that she was . . .

He got muddled, he spluttered, he had to control himself so that tears would not come to his eyes.

"You're a nice boy, Louis, very very decent. I'd like very much to see you again too, but don't come at the same time as today. It was just by chance that I didn't go to work this afternoon, because I had to see someone."

"Who?" he dared ask.

"Now don't be jealous! It would surprise you if I answered that it was my uncle who comes from Tours once a month and invites me out for lunch. He's a winegrower. My father was a winegrower too. He was one of the first killed in 1914."

"Like my brother-in-law."

"He was in the cavalry of the line."

"So was my brother-in-law."

"I usually work until seven or eight and since I have dinner in a restaurant on Place Saint-Georges, I'm hardly ever here before ten or so."

"What about mornings?"

"I sleep late. Then I wash and dress and make up and after that I do my marketing, because I prepare my own lunch."

"I start work at ten in the evening."

"Every evening?"

"Except Sunday."

"On Sunday I go to the country with girl friends."

"So?"

"Come and knock at my door from time to time around ten in the morning. You're not sleeping then?"

"I sleep just as well in the afternoon."

"It doesn't matter if you find me in bed tired-looking and with my face shiny. Might as well empty the bottle, don't you think?"

He drank a third glass and half of a fourth, and when she accompanied him to the landing he was very animated.

"It's a day that . . . a day that I . . . Don't you think I'm ridiculous?"

"No. But it's time you had dinner. Your mother's waiting for you."

He did not remember having told her that.

"All right, now go!"

And she looked at him pensively as he walked down the first flight.

He saw Louise again only twice. Each time he came with little cakes and a bottle of port. There were mornings when he left Les Halles feeling so sleepy that all he thought of was dropping into bed and did not even bother to lower the blind.

At other times, he was so eager to work on a painting that he could not get home fast enough.

The last time he went to see her, he did not feel that he was in form. He was acting from conviction. He rang the bell and waited. At first, there was no answer, though he heard voices inside. He rang again and there were footsteps. The door opened slightly and he caught sight of a man who had hastily slipped on Louise's blue bathrobe.

"What is it?"

"Nothing," he answered without insisting.

Nevertheless, a few months later he painted a picture that he entitled "Portrait of Louise." There was neither a face nor a body in it, only a window, a canary in a hanging cage, and, above the roofs of the Palais Royal, a sky of the softest and most dazzling blue he had ever obtained.

In October, a month before the famous Armistice Day, he feverishly awaited the evening conversation with his mother at the dinner table. He had a bad conscience, he felt like an executioner, he was ready to give in even before starting.

"I've got something to tell you, Mama."

"You getting married too?"

When he went away, Gabrielle would be the only one left in the apartment which had once been so full that everyone had to fight to defend his place.

"I'm not getting married. I don't think I ever will. I've found a studio. Wait! That doesn't mean I'm leaving you. What is it like now? We're never at home together except for dinner. Your working hours aren't the same as mine and we don't sleep at the same time. The studio will be the place where I work, you understand, the way Vladimir worked at M. Brillanceau's. Remember, Mama, you didn't spend any more time with Vladimir or the twins than you do with me."

"Where will you sleep?"

He blushed.

"First of all, I promise to come and have dinner with you every day. I'll spend my Sundays with you, either here or in my studio, where it'll be a pleasure to see you."

"Are you taking your bed?"

"If you don't mind. I feel like working more and more. I don't go to sleep until I'm knocked out."

"Where is it?"

"Not far from here, on Rue de l'Abbé-de-l'Epée."

"Is it expensive?"

"Thirty francs a month, with a toilet."

"Have you signed the lease?"

"I'll sign it tomorrow morning, if you allow me to."

"And what if I don't?" she exclaimed with a burst of laughter. "But of course, my little chick, of course I allow you to! Your wings and hackles have grown without my realizing it. And you, at the age of twenty, you blush at asking me to be free!"

"It's because of my painting, you understand?"

"Of course! Of course! It's always because of something."

She was not crying and did not seem sad.

"When are you moving?"

"Tomorrow I'll move my things, my painting material and my canvases."

"With my cart?"

"When you've finished work. I'll sleep here, and the day after tomorrow . . ."

He imagined how the room would look. His mother's bed in the middle of the big empty space would seem tiny. He did not yet realize how lucky he was. A month later, what with the return of the men who were still in the army, with the arrival of foreigners who were going to invade Paris and the painters who would congregate in Montparnasse, he would have found nothing equivalent to his studio without having to pay a small fortune.

It was in the yard of an old house, or rather an ancient house, not an old house like theirs. It must have been a private mansion in the past, and it had been kept in repair during its two or three centuries of existence. The walls were of stone. The spacious arch led to a cobbled yard in the middle of which stood a linden tree.

There were apartments only in the front part of the building. They were occupied by middle-class people, civil servants, a dentist, a young couple, of whom the husband was a prisoner in Germany and whose three- or four-year-old son played alone in the yard.

The low part of the building, at the rear of the yard, had no doubt been a stable in the past. It had been transformed into a glass-enclosed workshop that had been occupied for fifty years by the same craftsman, a cabinetmaker who had specialized in repairing old, precious furniture and whose clients had been the best antique dealers on Rue du Bac, Rue de Seine, and Rue Jacob.

"He died exactly a month ago, sir. I've been in the house only ten years, but he'd already been working at the back of the yard fifty years before and maybe even earlier. People say he was married for fifteen years and that from the day he became a widower no woman was ever seen entering his place, even to do the cleaning, because he preferred to do it himself."

The concierge spoke on in that vein as she showed him around.

"When I think that furniture was piled up to the ceiling and that now the place is empty.

"A nephew in the provinces, his only heir, didn't even bother coming to Paris for the funeral and had everything sent to the auction house, including a stove the like of which I've never seen, enormous, with bronze decorations, there was always a pot of glue heating on it.

"Look! He himself built this wall. It makes a nice room. Behind it is the toilet. He didn't call in workmen for that either.

"You're quiet, aren't you? You look as if you were. I wouldn't want one of those painters who invite friends and models at night and make a racket until dawn. You seem rather shy."

"You know, Mama, it even has electricity!"

Even in his wildest dreams he would not have imagined such luck. The next day, radiant with joy, he took his mother's push-cart and moved out his personal belongings, which did not weigh much. The following day, he took his bed apart and tried to center his mother's against the wall.

The concierge had given him an idea while chattering away. For several days he prowled around the rooms of the Paris auction house, obviously not those in which valuable paintings, jewels, and antique furniture were sold, but the rooms containing odds and ends. He ended by unearthing a cylindrical cast-iron stove which had escaped from some provincial station and which he got for a song, and a low armchair that had no style at all but in which he felt very comfortable.

He kept his promise to have dinner with his mother.

"You'll have to tell me how much I owe you for my meals."

"Don't be silly, Louis. I realize why they called you the little saint. Did I make you pay for the milk that came from my body?"

"This is different. If you had to keep feeding all your children . . ."

He felt like biting his tongue off. He had just said "all." Only three of the five were left. Nothing was known of Guy. Vladimir merely dropped in on her every now and then for a few minutes, while the same woman waited for him in the street.

Alice had written that, after thinking it over, she did not plan to return to Paris after the war, that she had sold the furniture in her apartment to her English subtenant, and that perhaps she would remarry in the near future. She did not send a photograph of her son François, about whom she merely said that he was in good health.

"Will you come Sunday, Mama? There won't be much furniture. I've bought only the necessary pots and pans. The kitchen is small, a kind of closet, but it has a gas ring."

She came, dressed in the clothes she wore when she went dancing Saturday nights. She looked at everything, sniffed the smell of varnish and old wood that lingered in the studio.

"It's nice," she admitted, more to say something pleasant than out of conviction.

"Did you see my linden tree?"

For he had incorporated it into his universe, without knowing that, like the old cabinetmaker, he would be living in its shade for fifty years and more.

162

"It looks big, but when I become a real painter I'll need room."

"Why don't you hang your pictures?"

The few canvases he had kept without scraping them down so as to use them again were on the floor, facing the wall:

"Later. They're not good enough. If I saw them all the time, I'd tear them up and might never paint again."

She went to the studio only rarely, not feeling at home there, even less than if Louis had been living with another woman. "I'm having a visitor Saturday night, a man who knows about painting. It's the one from whom I buy my colors, and he's given me advice. He's a friend of lots of painters and plans to set up as a picture dealer someday."

He did not suspect that in talking that way, quietly and with a smile in spite of his inner excitement, he was moving further away from Gabrielle than Vladimir and Alice had done.

Yet the studio was only a five-minute walk from Rue Mouffe-tard. His new street had the same kind of stores as those on the one he had left. Boulevard Saint-Michel, down which his mother pushed her cart every morning, was a few feet away, a few houses off. Just opposite were the trees, benches, and iron chairs of the Luxembourg Gardens.

"It's only nine o'clock, Mama. I have time to walk you home."

"Why should I make you go out of your way?"

He insisted. He was wrong, for that Sunday evening, with the stores closed, the windows of the apartments open and the people leaning on the window sill and looking out, he in turn felt like an outsider. It was no longer the street whose image was fixed in his memory, an image he needed, which must not be stolen from him. He had promised his mother to go home and have dinner with her every evening and he suddenly wondered whether he would have the courage to keep his word.

All at once, things began to happen fast. It began with the

visit of M. Suard, who was not surprised not to see paintings hanging on the walls.

"May I look?"

As chance would have it, he picked up "The Little Train from Arpajon," and his first reaction was one of surprise, perhaps agreeable surprise, perhaps disagreeable. For several minutes he kept looking back and forth from Louis to the painting, as if he were examining the relationship between a portrait and its model.

"The fact is . . . No! . . . I was about to say something silly . . . I'll put it in a different way . . . I don't suppose you've tried to reproduce reality . . ."

"Why?" asked Louis simply, though he was disturbed.

"You've tried to give an impression of Les Halles, haven't you?"

"Why Les Halles?"

"The little train . . . the shed on the left and that side of beef as big as the shed . . . the cabbages in the foreground . . ."

"I didn't try to paint Les Halles."

"Then what *did* you try to paint?"

"I don't know. I started with the little train. That's why I've called the picture 'The Little Train from Arpajon.' It might have been elsewhere, on a street, even on the Champs-Elysées."

"In a certain way, anything that's represented is real."

"Everything is real."

"Have you seen any of the work of Odilon Redon?"

"No."

"He too thinks that he paints reality, and in a sense he does. Do you dream much?"

"Not when I sleep."

"But you do dream?"

"I don't know. I walk. I sit down on a bench. I look."

"Thinking about what?"

"About nothing."

Was he going to reply, like Louis's first teacher, the one with the flabby mouth, that it was impossible to think about nothing?

"And this picture, this one here, what title have you given it?"

"You know, the titles I give my pictures, they're meant just for me. The way, at first, one gives one's children a name, or a nickname that changes later. This little canvas is called, in my mind, 'Portrait of Louise.' "

"Are you in love with her?"

"Not any more."

"Did she play an important part in your life?"

"Maybe. I think so. What I can't manage to get is a certain sparkle that I'm after, the quivering space between objects. You understand?"

"I understand. Monet spent his life trying to do that."

Louis felt a pang of disappointment. He would have liked to be the first to have had that ambition.

"But Monet tried to achieve that result with light. The object was unimportant."

"My cabbages, my beef, my little train are *very* important."

M. Suard seemed to be musing.

"You're an odd man. I ought to say an odd young man, because you're under twenty."

"I'll be twenty in December."

"Does your work at Les Halles tire you?"

"It takes up my time and obliges me to sleep part of the day."

"What's that picture, the one bigger than the others?"

"It's a painting I botched. A sketch. I intended to do it over, larger, like a fresco, when I had enough room and money."

He turned it around reluctantly, and M. Suard was even more surprised than at the sight of the first painting.

"Don't tell me the title. I want to guess. 'War.' Am I right?"

"I hesitated between 'War' and 'The Parade.' I may try it

again someday. The soldiers will remain naked, wearing helmets or peaked caps. I prefer the cap, because of the color."

"What will you substitute for the woman?"

So M. Suard had guessed that it was the monstrous female sex organ that bothered him. Did he also guess why?

"I don't know yet. Maybe the Arch of Triumph?"

"Do you need this one in order to start work on the other?"

"No. I'll work without looking at it. I know it by heart."

"Listen, Louis. Do you mind my calling you that?"

A few months later, M. Suard was to start addressing him by the familiar *tu,* but Louis never reciprocated and for many many years continued to call him M. Suard.

"Of course not. I'd be delighted."

"I'd like to buy this painting that you pretend to reject, which someday perhaps you will reject, but which I consider very important."

"Why?"

"You're an artist and you don't have to understand. Perhaps it's better for you not to understand too much. German Expressionists worked along the same lines. They were intellectuals who knew where they were going, who were trying to express an idea. Did you know, when you were painting the soldiers, that they would be marching toward a monumental sex organ?"

"No, I didn't."

"In your mind, toward what were they marching?"

"I don't know. At the draft board, we were naked. I added the rifle and the cap and instead of making us parade by the medical officer, I put in a lot more, in ranks."

"That woman . . . No! Don't answer. I'm not rich. I know painters who haven't exhibited yet. I buy a picture from them from time to time. Let me confess something. Just between you and me. I've stopped smoking and having apéritifs in order to buy another painting when the opportunity occurred. I offer you a hundred francs for it. Fifty this month and fifty next. If, let's say in five years, your paintings are worth more, I promise to pay you the difference.

"That's too much. I want to give it to you."

"I know what I'm doing. Here's fifty francs. Before coming here, I was sure I'd buy something from you, but I didn't suspect it would be such a painting."

"Why?"

" 'The Little Train from Arpajon' will have more success, not right away, but in a few years. You see, Louis, you're neither an Impressionist nor a Fauve nor a Cubist. You're not an amateur either. If, as I hope, you remain yourself, it'll be hard to classify you. I don't quite understand either, but you've got something."

"I can't manage to get down on canvas what I'd like to. I don't think I'll ever be able to."

"Do you have a piece of paper? It's raining and I want very much to take this painting with me."

One day, shortly thereafter, Louis was sleeping in broad daylight, as he was in the habit of doing. It would have cost too much to buy curtains for a glassed-in bay twenty-five feet long and twelve feet high.

Someone was pounding at his door, and he did not immediately enter the world of reality.

"M. Cuchas! M. Cuchas! Wake up!"

And the voice of the concierge literally screamed:

"The war's over!"

He thanked her without opening the door, for he was wearing only a shirt and underpants. An uproar, including singing and the blowing of instruments, could be heard coming from Boulevard Saint-Michel. He hesitated for a moment, barefooted on the cold floor, then went back to bed and fell asleep.

In the evening, he had difficulty in getting to Les Halles, where couples were dancing in the markets. There was no dancing in the shed on Rue Coquillière, and M. Samuel, whose stom-

ach overflowed his trousers as usual, did not say a single un-
necessary word. His face was ashen. He had just learned that
his son had died of Spanish influenza at a military hospital in
Amiens.

M. Samuel was to die later, in the midst of work, in the midst
of the crowd, in the midst of the hubbub, of a stroke of apo-
plexy.

Former employees who had been demobilized were entitled
to their old jobs. The firm had been bought by two partners who
knew nothing about the business and who began by not allow-
ing pushcarts, which they considered a nuisance and unprofita-
ble, to enter the shed.

The peddlers of Rue Mouffetard scattered and either chose
another wholesaler or preferred to prowl about looking for bar-
gains.

Gabrielle was among the latter, so Louis no longer saw her
during the night or at dawn.

He had left the glass office and gone back to the blackboard.
At times he was so tired as a result of painting most of the day
that he would get mixed up in the figures that were called out to
him.

One of the partners, who had made a lot of money in scrap
metal, was particularly foulmouthed and had picked Louis as
scapegoat. His name was Smelke and it was hard to identify his
foreign accent.

M. Suard, who had paid the remainder of the hundred francs,
had taken "The Little Train from Arpajon" to show it to two or
three collectors whom the painting might interest. He was beginning to build up a clientele, not of rich people who bought, in
galleries, the work of established artists but of people who cared
enough about painting to buy pictures with the little extra
money they had, doctors, lawyers, storekeepers, clerks.

"I'm ashamed to tell you, Louis. Among the people I know,
there's only one who's interested, but he can't give more than
eighty francs."

"That's a lot, isn't it?"

"If I were you, I wouldn't accept."

"What if it made it possible for me to quit my job at Les Halles?"

"Well, in that case it's different."

"The Little Train from Arpajon" also was gone. A time was to come when full-size reproductions of it could be bought in most bookstores, not only in France but in foreign countries as well, even in America. The exact price of the reproduction was eighty francs.

IV

HOW LONG DID he continue having dinner at his mother's home almost every day? The answer to that question, as to many others, depended on the period in which he wondered about it, for time seemed longer to him at the age of forty than at sixty. Events were placed in such or such a period, but their chronological order would sometimes vary.

His mother, who was to live on until after the Second World War, kept making a reproach which he felt he did not deserve.

"If you'd stayed with me, if you'd kept coming to see me, I wouldn't be here with that lunatic and would have stayed on good old Rue Mouffetard just as my mother did until she died."

In 1945 she was living in a smart-looking cottage at Joinville, on the bank of the Marne.

"Léon's getting more and more impossible. Imagine, at his age and mine, he's becoming jealous. When he goes fishing, he fishes from in front of the house so as to keep an eye on me."

She was over seventy and the Léon in question, her second husband, was six or seven years older. He did not look his age.

He stood as straight, his shoulders were as broad and his flesh as firm as when Louis had met him for the first time.

Like the twins in the past, he had a square face and his hair was closely cropped, but it was all white.

Louis was sure that he had continued to have dinner alone with his mother for a long time and he could see himself bringing, when he had a little money, a dish that they were not in the habit of eating, a lobster, scallops in a shell, which had simply to be reheated, a cold chicken, a bottle of good wine or a small can of fat goose liver.

Guy's letter dated from late 1919 or early 1920, and Louis and his mother had been sitting at the table. Léon had not yet entered the picture when she had taken it out of her bag.

"It's strange, Louis. You'll see. It's not his handwriting, but he signed it."

On the envelope were several Ecuadorian stamps.

"Dear Mama,

"I suppose that now that the war has been over for some time, letters are no longer censored and I can write to you without getting you into trouble. You'll be surprised to receive this letter, which I hope finds you all in good health. Excuse me for not writing to you myself. You know I was never very good in spelling since I didn't spend much time in school.

"I have no news of Olivier or anyone else. I don't know if Olivier married his little Bedouin and if he still lives in Oran. When I left him, he spoke of joining the Foreign Legion or the African Battalions. I hope he didn't do such a foolish thing.

"Maybe you'll find the city of Guayaquil on a map of South America. It's almost opposite the Galápagos Islands. Do you remember that at home Olivier and I often used to talk about the Galápagos Islands and you didn't believe me when I said there were huge turtles hundreds of years old and so big that two persons could sit on them?

171

"Well, they exist. Olivier and I left with the idea of living on a desert island. Unfortunately, the boat on which we stowed away stopped off in Algeria, where we were discovered. Then we dreamed of making enough money to leave from Dakar.

"We worked as laborers and at other jobs. Olivier met a little girl who begged in the street.

"I admit that, for a Bedouin, she was very beautiful. Those people generally live in the mountains and are very proud.

"I wonder how that one landed in Oran and why she held out her hand in the street, with her eyes covered with flies.

"Olivier didn't want to go on. We argued and I went away alone. I got to Panama, which is a funny country, where I got a job on a freighter going down the Pacific coast.

"I won't go into detail because it would take time and I had lots of adventures and hardships. If I started telling my life history, poor Dorothy would never finish writing this letter that I'm dictating to her. She's very educated. She's English and was born in Quito, the capital of Ecuador, where her father was consul.

"He made her go to school first in Quito, then in Panama, where there's an American school, and after that he sent her to England, where she studied the natural sciences.

"She's begging me, while I'm dictating this letter, not to talk about her so much and I'm sure she's writing down everything I say. She even worked for quite a long time at the museum. When she came back here, she was on a kind of mission.

"I was still trying to get to the Galápagos. I would have had to rent a boat and I didn't have enough money. I worked as an elevator boy in a hotel, because they built an eight-story hotel. I managed to get along until I met Dorothy, who's eight years older than I.

"We were married in a few minutes by an English clergyman, so I've become a Protestant, but it's of no importance to either Dorothy or me.

"I still don't understand how she could have fallen in love with a big brute who can hardly write and whom she had to teach everything.

"We now live in a bungalow, which means a wooden house, very comfortable, with all improvements, twenty miles out of town. Since the road doesn't go any farther, we live right in the brush.

"It's hotter than in Africa. Plants grow amazingly fast and you'll be surprised to hear that we earn our living hunting butterflies, hummingbirds, and egrets, which we send to New York and London where we sell them at very high prices.

"There are also certain lizards and certain birds that we catch alive and that zoos fight to get.

"Dorothy attends to the correspondence and goes with me into the brush, where you have to be very careful not only because of the jaguars but particularly the insects.

"We have a comfortable life. Three half-breeds look after the bungalow and prepare our meals. I speak Spanish and English almost better than French. The thing that makes me sad is that I won't ever be able to go to see you in France, where I'd be arrested as a deserter.

"I hesitated when I learned that war was declared. The consul would have paid my fare. He was angry with me when he realized that I preferred to stay here, and for years he pretended not to recognize me.

"He has forgotten about it by now, calls me Troublemaker, and only last week came to our house for whisky. Dorothy and I have no children. Let us have news about all of you. The address is at the bottom of the page. San José is the name of the nearest village.

"I kiss you with all my love. Forgive me for having gone away. I couldn't help it.

"Your loving son,
"Guy"

At the age of more than seventy-five, Gabrielle still kept the letter in the cooky box, which she had taken with her to Joinville. The Léon incident had occurred later, Louis was sure of it, in 1921 or 1922. She was still going to Les Halles. He had gone to see her at home one Sunday morning, at about ten o'clock, for she did not like either his studio or his paintings. He had found her in undress, sitting opposite a man touched with gray who seemed to be quite at home.

"Don't go away, Louis. It's not what you think. I want you to meet Léon, Léon Hanet. He's a foreman in a big plumbing firm on Boulevard Voltaire. He's been a widower for ten years and has two married daughters. One of them's the wife of a doctor."

The man was wearing only trousers, a white collarless shirt, and a pair of old shoes on his sockless feet.

Gabrielle laughed with embarrassment.

"Imagine, Léon has got it into his head that he wants to marry me. He makes a good living and wants me to give up my pushcart."

She in turn was betraying Rue Mouffetard, like the rest of the clan. The others had gone off, of course, but it had never occurred to Louis that she would not remain in their home.

"He has a nice apartment on Boulevard Richard-Lenoir. What do you think of the idea? Even though I keep telling him that I'm too old . . ."

She had remarried, discreetly, without telling anyone, and their former home was invaded by a family of Poles.

Later on, newspaper articles and even biographies of him related that during the long years when his work had been unappreciated he had never had enough to eat and that he had hunted for food in garbage cans.

It was untrue. The legend grew out of the fact that he had once spoken of the couple he had seen from the window on Rue Mouffetard. He had added that he had later been curious to know what edible food was to be found in garbage cans and had opened two or three as he walked by.

As for hunger, he attached no importance to it. He had never been gluttonous. Even when he had money, he would be satisfied with milk, hard-boiled eggs, and cheese. There were times, it is true, when he had to do without. Not for years, but occasionally.

There was also a tendency to include him among what was called the Montparnasse painters, who had invaded the fourteenth district after the war and who could be seen and heard, talking all languages, first at the Rotonde and on the terrace of the Dôme and later at the Coupole.

These cafés were frequented not only by painters and sculptors in odd getups, men and women alike, but also by writers, poets and critics whom, before long, tourists came to gape at.

Louis had spent a few hours a day over a period of a month in a corner of the Rotonde, sitting in front of a cup of coffee and milk without ever saying a word to anyone.

He had recognized well-known painters there, men who, especially toward the end, always arrived accompanied by a court of aesthetes and pretty girls. Some of them had conspicuous cars which would be surrounded by rubbernecks.

Louis had not been involved in any group. Nobody in Montparnasse knew his name. He was only a short, thin young man with tousled hair and a contented smile.

M. Suard had left the stationery store on Rue de Richelieu too late or too soon. Too late because in 1923 or 1924 there were as many picture galleries as night clubs in Montparnasse, to say nothing of the larger and more luxurious ones that sprang up on Rue du Faubourg-Saint-Honoré.

The value of money had changed. Formerly, when Louis lived with his mother, people counted by sous. Now they counted by hundreds and thousands of francs, and artists whom no one would mention in ten years were selling their paintings at prices higher than those paid for works by an Italian master of the Renaissance.

M. Suard had also started too soon, because people had not yet begun, as was to happen later, to distinguish between what would last and what would end up at the Flea Market.

Rue de Seine was not a bad location, but the narrow show window with the dark green frame was stuck between a butcher shop whose marble counters were covered with poultry and a modest fruit and vegetable store whose baskets and crates extended, as on Rue Mouffetard, to the middle of the sidewalk.

Passers-by did not notice that between the two was a picture gallery, especially since the paintings that were shown and the posters that occasionally announced an exhibition bore unknown names.

It was to that period that journalists and others alluded later when they wrote that Cuchas had lived in poverty for years.

As a matter of fact, it did go on for years, with ups and downs, until 1927 or 1928. In order to carry on, M. Suard sold some of his furniture and moved from his apartment at the Porte d'Orléans to a cheaper one.

When he saw Louis enter the gallery with a canvas under his arm, he was torn between enthusiasm and his despair at not having money to give him.

"Are you at the end of your rope?"

Louis would smile and shake his head.

"There's someone interested who's supposed to come back on Monday. I'm sure he'll be back. He's excited by one of your canvases, 'The Baskets,' but I refused to let him have it cheap. Now's the time we've got to establish your reputation, and if I sell you for less than the others no one will take you seriously."

The bowl was full, half full, or empty, depending on the month or the week. It was a big ceramic bowl that had been used for God knows what. There was no way of telling what craftsman had fired it, in what kiln, and how he had obtained that bright metallic red which had caught Louis's eye at the Flea Market in Saint-Ouen, where he sometimes roamed about on Sundays.

He had placed it on a shelf, for the studio had gradually become cluttered with tables, stands, easels, objects that interested no one, glass paperweights in which one could see snow falling, odd-shaped bottles of all colors—in short, a collection of odds and ends, which he called his treasure.

The bowl in the studio played the role of his mother's cooky box. When he came home with a little money, Cuchas would put it into the bowl, whether it was in change or bills.

"See whether there's enough left in the bowl to buy some salami," he would say, without stopping his painting.

There was often a woman with him. He had built, with his own hands, a narrow couch, for he hated to sleep with anyone.

He had never been able to say no and everyone regarded his smile, his way of tilting his head, as an acceptance.

"I bet you're a painter, aren't you?"

He wore the same suit for ten years. It was made of a kind of corduroy that had been used for laborers' trousers when he was a child. He had not chosen it in order to look like a painter but because he had always wanted such a suit. Otherwise, clothes did not matter to him and he sometimes wore the same shirt for two weeks.

"You have a look in your eyes that women must find attractive."

He did not believe it. He didn't care. He let them have their way. They would follow him home. Three cats had taken refuge in his studio, and he accepted a woman's presence as he did theirs.

He rather liked seeing a naked body moving about in the light that streamed in through the big window. But because of the complaints of a tenant whose apartment faced the yard, he had to have a curtain, and one day, when there was money in the bowl, he had one made of the cheapest material he could find, burlap.

He was neither poor nor rich. He spent his time painting, in quest of the sparkling space that he had been seeking so long and that he continued to seek all his life.

Some girl friends stayed two days, others a month or more. For a time, there were two Lesbians, one of them a Swede, who had no place to sleep. They were fond of him, especially the Swede, whom he seemed to fascinate and who compared him to a Scandinavian elf.

Why did Cuchas suddenly think of Pliska one day when Suard, who was discouraged, spoke of giving up his gallery? He had run into the Czech again a few nights before on the terrace of the Dôme amidst a group of people talking different languages. He was the biggest and strongest of the party and had such a booming voice that despite the noise in the street he could be heard at the other end of the terrace.

"You ask my first name? . . . No first name . . . Only Pliska . . . Pliska . . . You all hear . . ."

Though he was drunk, he nevertheless recognized Louis, to whom he called his audience's attention.

"Ask my friend . . . Knew him child . . . Him know Pliska great sculptor . . . Greatest sculptor in world . . . Him have seen 'Couple' . . . No more 'Couple' . . . Changed name . . . 'Procreation' . . . eh! . . . 'Procreation' . . . Understand? . . ."

This "Procreation," which was to make Pliska famous and really launch the Suard Gallery, not on Rue de Seine but on Rue la Boétie, attracted the attention of an American art critic who had been commissioned by a Philadelphia millionaire to buy the best works of painting and sculpture he could find for the collector's private museum, which he intended to bequeath to his city.

That was how one of Cuchas's small canvases, entitled "The

Wedding," happened to cross the Atlantic on the same boat as the Czech's monument.

Around the age of thirty, Louis became plump, and his cheekbones filled out and slightly dulled his features. He ate almost every day at the Caves d'Anjou, a restaurant with a tin counter and cane-bottomed chairs that was frequented by truck drivers. He would always sit in the same corner, for he liked corners and felt too conspicuous or vulnerable in the middle of a room.

"A glass of white wine, M. Cuchas?"

The carroty cat would jump on his knees and he would stroke it mechanically. He drank little, two or three glasses of white wine a day, walked the streets, and would stop to look at a piece of wall or watch workmen on a scaffold. He liked benches, especially those in the little parks or small squares where there was almost never anyone and where he could sit for two hours without being aware of the passing of time.

Suard was beginning to get better prices for his paintings and the bowl was almost always full.

"Is that where you keep your money?"

"It's beautiful, isn't it? I've never managed to get the same red."

"Anyone can dip into it."

He shrugged. Money or no money, his life remained the same. At times when he prowled about Rue Mouffetard, he looked as if he were walking around a magic circle.

For a long time he had been inside it and he seemed to hesitate to re-enter it. Hadn't he picked the Caves d'Anjou at the corner of Rue Rataud because it was at the frontier of his former universe?

Vladimir was living between Marseilles and Toulon. He had a car that stopped at the studio two or three times. He was more ironic and aggressive than in the past and there was a certain disquieting heaviness in his gaze.

"Have you seen Mama?"

"I have. I don't like her guy."

"They're married."

"I know."

"So is Alice. She married a cattle dealer and claims she's happy."

She too came to see him, though without her husband or children, for she had had two more since her second marriage.

"Are you in Paris alone?"

"No, all five of us came for the Automobile Show."

She had put on weight. Her gaze was lusterless.

"We're building a new house, a villa, two miles from Nevers. My husband's buying up all the grassland he can find. It's the best investment. I'm going to see Mama tomorrow."

"Do you have her address?"

"She sent it to me on a postcard."

"She's remarried."

"It's funny, isn't it? I'd have been embarrassed at her age."

He would sometimes work on a painting for five or six hours at a stretch and then toss away his brush and throw himself down on his bed to cry.

Pliska encouraged him. Every time he came he was accompanied by a new girl whom he ordered, as soon as she opened her mouth:

"You not talk . . . Not know . . . Only screw . . ."

He would examine the paintings one by one, carefully, with his brows knit. He was deeply moved one day when he caught sight of the box of colored pencils he had given little Louis one Christmas Day.

"You keep?"

They were almost intact, having been used only for drawing the tree in the schoolyard and for two or three childish sketches. The dark blue one was missing. His sister had taken it one evening to copy the pattern of a skirt from a fashion magazine.

Since then he had painted another tree, the linden in the yard, "Mr. Tree."

"Why Mister?"

What could he answer? He smiled, slightly embarrassed.

"I don't know."

It had been the same with cabbages. He had painted lots of cabbages. Most people eat vegetables without ever having watched a cabbage or leek or young carrot actually live.

"Do you find cabbages decorative?"

"No. Not decorative."

Journalists began coming to question him.

"Is it a memory from the time when you worked at Les Halles?"

"I don't know."

One day when he was attending the opening of another painter's exhibition at the Suard Gallery, a voice cried out:

"Well, what do you know! The little saint!"

A man put out his hand. Louis tried in vain to attach a name to the face, which he nevertheless knew very well.

"Don't you remember? Randal. Raoul Randal, the one who beat you up because of a yellow marble. Is this your exhibition?"

"No."

"I was told you'd become a painter. How's it going?"

He looked him up and down as if to judge the degree of his success from his face and clothes.

"I'm working."

"Do you sell?"

"Sometimes."

"That's good. What does this bird do? I don't know anything about art. I received an invitation because I've put some money into a small weekly."

A journalist who had heard the conversation came over.

"Why did you call him the little saint?"

"Cuchas? Because at school he let everyone beat him up without complaining to the teacher.

"Or maybe because he used to help his mother push her cart to Les Halles and back at three in the morning. She was a peddler. They were very poor. If I remember right, there were two twins, older than he. They were nasty little cusses."

Louis did not protest. He kept smiling, as he had smiled in the past when he was slapped or kicked. The story appeared in an evening paper, which the concierge brought him. She was all excited.

"Now I understand, those cats you keep, those girls who take whatever they want."

The legend spread. Before the second war, many people were calling him the little saint and caricatures of him appeared with a halo around his head.

Until the age of forty-two he had never had any desire to travel and it was only when people began to leave Paris, when the Germans were expected to arrive any hour, that he left for the south. One of his collectors, a doctor, drove him as far as Moulins but went no farther because his wife had relatives there and it was unthinkable that the Germans would get as far as that. Louis got a few lifts from truck drivers and also walked part of the way. In Lyons, after waiting on the platform a night and a day, he was able to get into a train that took him to Cannes, where he was unable to find a room.

The sight of the sea thrilled him. However, he was obliged to go a bit north, first to Mougins, then to Mouans-Sartoux, a real village without villas or hotels for tourists, a few miles from Grasse.

He spent the war years there. He no more read the papers than he had done during the first war. He rented a shanty which he used as a studio. Suard and his family had settled in Nice.

"Well, do you find the light bright enough and the colors pure enough?"

"I thought I did at first."

For two years he had been trying to render the vividness of nature.

"You no longer think so?"

"The light eats everything up, it chokes everything. All that's left is a kind of mush. I'd have done better to stay in Paris."

"We'll be there before long. Here, take this! I've brought you a bit of butter that some friends sent me."

Before long . . . No . . . It lasted another three years. Suard was selling his paintings at such high prices that Louis did not know what to do with the money. People were afraid of a devaluation and were buying anything.

"Do you want me to keep it for you?"

"I don't care."

He had his corner in the local inn, the smell of which delighted him. His stoutness had gone and never came back. In fact, when he returned to his studio in Paris, where he was surprised to find every object in its place, he began to get lean. His hair, which remained fine and loose, had turned gray. It flitted about his face and made him look thinner and more delicately modeled than when he was a child.

There were paintings of his in many museums. People were surprised to find him in that comfortless studio where he did not even want to have a telephone. He continued to wear corduroy suits, though he could no longer find the thick, warm, strong cloth of the old days.

His grandmother had died. His mother and her husband were still living in the cottage at Joinville. Nobody in the family was left on Rue Mouffetard, and when he went back to it he recognized few faces. M. Stieb was dead. So were the Dorés. The old house was still there, but a six-story building was under construction next to it.

"You're Louis Cuchas, aren't you, the half-brother of a man named Joseph Heurteau?"

He almost said no, because of the unfamiliar "Joseph."

"Do you mean Vladimir?"

"So you know his nickname?"

"He was called that when I was born."

"Why?"

"I don't know."

That was in 1960. His hair was now white and his features had become so pure that it was as if he were disembodied and were only a limpid gaze, a gentle, disquieting smile.

Two men had come to his studio and shown him their police badges.

"How long is it since you've seen him?"

"The last time was in Cannes, during the war."

"What was he doing?"

"I don't know."

"Didn't you ask him what he lived on?"

"No."

"Did he spend a lot of money?"

"I don't know."

"Didn't you notice that he hung around with shady characters?"

"He was alone with his wife. I happened to run into him in a café."

"Do you mind if we look around your studio?"

They searched everywhere, methodically. One of them admitted in discouragement:

"We didn't find anything at your mother's place either."

"What are you looking for?"

"Dope. Joseph Heurteau, known as Vladimir, is one of the top big-shots in the dope racket in France. He was run in for pimping, but now we want to give him the works."

He heard nothing more about Vladimir for a year. He was almost at the point of making the objects on his canvas vibrate by surrounding them with air or light. Almost. Not quite. It would take years.

He learned from his mother that Vladimir had been sentenced to fifteen years of hard labor.

He continued to paint all day long. In most of his paintings there were traces of his mother, his sister Alice, and even little Emilie. Nobody noticed it. The faces of the redheads also appeared several times, as did the stove, a yellow marble, the bedsheet with a hole in it that had separated the mattresses from Gabrielle's bed.

He would soon be seventy and walked with short steps, conscious of his fragility.

In the evening, he liked to sit in a neighborhood movie house amidst the warm crowd. When early films were shown he discovered the actors of the time when he was a young man and had hardly been aware of the existence of the cinema.

He had worked a great deal. He was still working. It would take him years more to render what he felt had always been in him.

"What exactly is your aim?"

"I don't know."

That was the sentence that he had uttered most often in the course of his life and which he kept repeating.

M. Suard was dead. His son, who had taken over the gallery, called him Maître. Many people called him Maître.

He remembered the evening when he had thought he saw a slight cloud come over his mother's face, which had always been radiant. One of the twins was dead. Emilie was dead. Pretty Alice was fat and callous. She too was clouded over. And Vladimir had no chance of getting out of prison alive. Only one of them was left, far away, in Ecuador, and he had stopped writing. He was nearing seventy-five and his wife was over eighty. Were they still alive and were they still hunting for butterflies and birds of paradise?

At times he thought he could feel the cloud coming over him

too. He would think of the mattresses, of Emilie's cot, of Rue Mouffetard, of the pushcarts arriving at Les Halles.

Had he not taken something from everything and everyone? Had he not used their substance?

He didn't know, he mustn't know, otherwise he would be unable to carry on to the end.

He continued to walk with little steps, to smile.

"May I ask you, Maître, how you see yourself?"

He did not reflect very long. His face lit up for a moment as he said, joyously and modestly:

"As a small boy."

Epalinges, October 13, 1964